JR

NP

Secret Places

By the same author

CAVE WITH ECHOES

THE SOMNAMBULISTS

THE GODMOTHER

THE BUTTERCUP CHAIN

THE SINGING HEAD

ANGELS FALLING

THE KINDLING

A STATE OF PEACE

PRIVATE LIFE

HEAVEN ON EARTH

A LOVING EYE

THE HONEY TREE

SUMMER PEOPLE

For children

THE BIRTHDAY UNICORN

ALEXANDER IN THE LAND OF MOG

Secret Places

Janice Elliott

ST. MARTIN'S PRESS
NEW YORK

The lines of poetry on page 14 are taken from *Rendezvous* by Alan Seeger. This was published in a collection of his poems by Constable & Company in 1917. Those on page 51 are taken from *Death's men* by W. J. Turner from *Selected Poems 1916–36*, reproduced by permission of Mrs J. F. Lisle and the Oxford University Press.

Library of Congress Catalog Card Number: 81-51421

ISBN   0-312-70871-8
First Edition

For my father
Douglas Elliott

. . . Mais le temps la dissoudra comme les autres, et tu ne sauras plus rien de moi, jusqu'au jour où mes pas s'arrêteront et où s'envolera de moi une dernière petite ombre . . . qui sait où?

Colette

Part One

I

'This is Laura. She has come from Abroad,' said Miss Trott.

Patience always remembered Laura Meister, the first day she arrived as a new girl and came into the classroom late, in the middle of the afternoon. And she was skinny and rather sallow and wearing a non-uniform frock – a sort of frilled pinafore with bib and puffed sleeves. She had little gold studs in her ears and a locket round her neck. Outside it was the weary tail-end of an English winter, inside, chalk-dust, boredom, Miss Trott pinching her nose with a lawn handkerchief no bigger than a sigh. The fumes of her paraffin stove and the pointlessness of Latin: Julia with her *mensa* in her *casa*. The smell of school dinner remembered swedes and it seemed there would be no deliverance ever, then in came Laura, improperly dressed.

The class waited for Trotty to blow up, but all the teacher said was: 'This is Laura. She has come from Abroad.' And to Laura: 'We are attempting the tongue of Virgil. I regret that for this afternoon you must share a book. Patience Mackenzie?'

'Yes, Miss Trott?'

'If you were to move a little to the left, I believe you could make room for Laura.'

They might have known. Trotty always put drama in its place. Once, Posy Potter had had a fit, she fell off her chair on to the ground, foaming, and Trotty just shoved an india-rubber between her teeth, sent someone for matron and carried on.

It was the same with the war. When school assembled for the first term after the outbreak and found Miss Trott was their form-mistress as well as their Latin and History teacher, all she said was: 'I hope you have your gas-masks. The fire alarm will be used for shelter practice and prefects will mark major battles on the wall map in the hall. It is regrettable but I wish to hear no more about it.'

There was something though, about Laura's arrival, that even Trotty could not quite defuse. Nothing had happened and yet the weather in the room had changed.

So far Laura had not spoken. If she was foreign, it was possible even that she did not speak English. Perhaps they would converse in Latin? Patience smiled and pointed to the lesson they were working on. *The wagon was full of olives and the blue water delighted the happy sailor. Good farmer, your anger is great. Many are the tears of your daughter. The Italians love the blue sky of their Italy. Great horses plough the broad fields of Britain*. Upper Five B is playing netball in the rain. Inside her text-book Patience has written: Patience Mackenzie, Upper Four T, Albert Lodge School for Girls, England, Europe, the World, the Universe. *I plough my fields* – she shows Laura Meister in the crib at the back – *and I give water to my vineyards*.

She should not have shown Laura the crib. The Trot is all-seeing but they are saved by the bell.

'Thank you very much,' said Laura, 'for helping me.' Her voice was low and almost accentless, but there was something formal about her inflections, as though she had learned English from a book. Well, she probably had. It was the same with her manner: she addressed Patience with a strange, old-fashioned politeness. Then she gathered up her pencil-case – an expensive-looking wooden one, decorated with hearts and flowers – and walked quickly from the room without looking to either side. When the rest got down to the subterranean cloakroom, she was gone.

The girls in their navy gaberdine raincoats and velour hats, satchels and gas-masks swinging, trailed towards the tram stop. The gutters ran black with rain, they would get home in the dark but, having looked forward to this moment all day, they found themselves, as so often, reluctant to part – as though the shared experience of school, however detested, had made of them a company. Each night this comradeship was broken, each day renewed. It was in some ways an unnatural arrangement, they often resented it, but never, oddly, did any one of them question this ordering of their lives. The school was there. It simply was.

Nina Cherry wore her hat with the brim turned up and had been the first to sport a brassière. She met the Boys' High School in the Arboretum and was rather dashing. She was their expert on Fashion and Life.

'Did you see that *frock*! I mean, it was a pinny! How could her parents let her out like that?'

'Perhaps she has no parents?' said Rose Delane, dreamily – always so sweet, so soft, remembering people's birthdays and crying at flowers and representations of the Virgin.

'Of course she has parents. Everyone has.' They had reached the tram stop now and Barbara Baxter – whose shirt never came out of her skirt, even playing hockey – decided this was a day she would be irritated by Rose Delane. 'You're very silly sometimes, Rose.'

Posy Potter – bespectacled and mouse-like, not at all the sort of person you would expect to have fits – suggested: 'Perhaps it's because she comes from Abroad?'

No one ever took any notice of Posy Potter.

So far Patience had said nothing. She shivered and suddenly would have been, if she could at this moment, home by her own fireside, curtains drawn, comfortably bored, her father come in and the door locked behind him, everything sure and predictable, contained. But the rain was coming down hard now and a pair of steaming dray-horses from the local brewery held up the traffic. On the pavements people looked pinched, wan, driven, every soul scuttling to his burrow. And Barbara was saying, scornfully: 'Well, if you want to know about her, you'd better ask Patti. She's going to be Laura Meister's best friend.'

Something to do with the brewery drays. That night Patience Mackenzie dreamed of a field, that was apparently England, and great horses yoked to a heavy plough; she saw their plumes of breath and felt the cold of iron, sometimes she steered the plough and sometimes ran before it and fell. And hunched, her cheek against the earth, waiting for the hoofs and then the iron, she saw into the secrets of furrows where the earth had been turned once already, throwing up small flowers and stones, fossil and flint, history, private things. In the morning there was a frost, cold as iron.

The school was there. It simply was. In 1855 James Fleet, a lace-maker of this city, had fallen upon fat times and commissioned Julius Mildenburg, architect of Lyons, to build for him a fine house in the style of a French château. Somewhere on the way via Calais, Julius, always an Anglophile, had been seized by reverence for the present queen. (It was said even that he visited Osborne by yacht and on the foreshore came upon Britain's consort. It was a wet and windy day and the Solent was disagreeable but Mildenburg wished a good morning to his Highness. Who remarked that this historic stretch of water brought him to mind of the bay of Naples. Mildenburg thought that the Consort looked tired but they walked for a while on the shore and Julius made notes on his cuff that a marriage between Anglo-German romantic practicality and French reason might bring to architecture her crown.)

Hence, Albert Lodge; though by the time it was done its royal patron, the Prince, had given up his salt-blown walks and gone unexpectedly under the earth. Soon after, James Fleet followed him, for reasons unrecorded, cutting his throat in the very conservatory that was now an adjunct to the library; still known as the conservatory though the flowers were long gone and schoolgirls now bloomed where James Fleet had once poured out his life's blood on his prize camellias. And he left behind him rather a monster of a place, a passionate and domestically impossible compromise that had faithfully observed and digested a number of styles and taken the worst from each. So the turret where the sixth-form study kept itself was unbearably cold and the fine bay windows faced north. In another climate the terrace giving onto the Arboretum would have been wonderful. When the Girls' School Trust took over in 1880, a number of the mouldings were found to be obscene – nymphs and shepherds capering a little wantonly were threatened but not re-moved. Greek had now become a part of the enlightened syllabus and the mouldings were designated classical by one of the remarkable ladies who pioneered female education by simply getting on with the job. She had walked through Greece in sensible shoes, taking now and then to donkeys, seen the Parthenon and was related to Elgin.

But this was not the school the girls knew, because no one had ever told them. They did not know that the iron railing around the balcony was wrought in one of James Fleet's most cherished lace designs. Only in the forbidden entrails of the building, that housed the ancient and dangerous boiler, were they aware dimly that this place had a powerful and relentless history. And they were drawn here, breaking rules, because they were curious, and they were cold.

Also, within the elaborate structure of the school, this was the one forbidden place to which, by tacit understanding and a horror of cobwebs, the authorities chose mostly to turn a blind eye.

No one questioned this – just as it never occurred to anyone that, in an objective sense, the school did not exist. What was it, when you came down to it, but a fantasy in a way? A flimsy tissue of rules, a conspiracy between those who obey and those who are obeyed – of whom the first far outnumbered the second. Yet hardly anyone thought seriously of challenging those rules.

Did James Fleet cut his throat all over his camellias because for one fatal moment he saw his great adventure in stone as fantasy? Huff and puff and you could blow it all down.

The only real danger in the basement boiler-room was old Bill, who tended his precious monster, chewed tobacco, spat great gobs and blew his nose with his fingers. There were rumours that he was a rapist.

They waited until he had gone then inspected Posy Potter's chilblains. Posy was only interesting, really, for her fits and her chilblains. 'Show us your chilblains, Posy,' Barbara Baxter would say, with the authority of one whose mother was a doctor. And, blushing, Posy would undo her suspenders and slip down her woollen stockings to reveal her poor mottled feet. Patience Mackenzie wondered sometimes if Posy had fits because that was the only way – chilblains apart – she could get anyone to take notice of her?

Today, however, the chilblain inspection was cursory: the boiler-room conclave had something else on their minds.

'I think,' said Rose Delane, 'that she's a refugee.'

'Or a spy?' Nina Cherry suggested hopefully.

They pondered the possibilities, sharing Posy Potter's Mars Bar.

'We don't even know where she's from.'

'It's no use asking Trotty.'

'What sort of name is Laura Meister?'

'Foreign.'

'Everyone knows *that*.'

'There's only one thing for it: Patti will have to ask her.'

'I'm not sure I want to. I don't think I care very much. If you'll shut up, I've got to do my prep.'

Of course, Patience was far from indifferent to Laura Meister. In fact, it was to hide the intensity of her interest in the new girl that she dissembled. Passion is dangerous, it betrays, leaves one vulnerable, so instinctively Patience – by nature an open person – actually avoided Laura for several days. Something about this odd girl disturbed her in a way she could not understand and even resented. Why did she wear that stupid pinafore? The locket? The gold ear-studs? Why didn't she play hockey?

Patience decided to be ordinary, stick with her crowd and work hard. Miss Lowrie, who took English and Drama, and was young and really quite beautiful, with sad weeping eyes and floating scarves, praised Patti's essay and lent her a book of Great War poets. Patience smuggled it home and read it at night with a torch under the bedclothes. *I have a rendezvous with Death/At some disputed barricade/When Spring comes back with rustling shade/And apple-blossoms fill the air – /I have a rendezvous with Death/When Spring brings back blue days and fair.* Patience didn't quite understand that, except that it was about death and it made her feel dizzy, rather delicious. And she knew that Miss Lowrie had put another burden on her – one more secret to keep.

Winter returned. There was a spit of snow, though it didn't lie.

'Are you reading in bed, Patience?' called her mother. Patience switched off the torch and lay in the blacked-out dark. She heard her

14

parents going to bed. They talked for a long time and their murmur soothed her. She let the book slip to the floor and played a familiar childhood game: imagining this room to contain the world, or all the world that was necessary to her. She felt, though she could not see, the shapes of the furniture: dresser, desk, chair, wardrobe. Dolls she'd long grown out of but couldn't sack. Being ill in this room and being safe, surfacing from a slight fever as warm and soft as a pigeon. Falling back. Strange, elaborate dreams, then her mother flinging open the curtain and the sun streaming in. 'There, you're better then, aren't you.' A brown boiled egg in a blue egg-cup then, as now, sleep. But Pluto had watched the girl when she was wandering through the meadows. Soon he will have snatched the frightened girl. Where has Ceres wandered now? Then Patience's father was called up and her mother cried. *Often our brothers love war but our sisters always long for peace.*

Miss Trott gave Laura a note to take home and that was the end of the pinafore. Rose Delane had a new theory: that Trotty was being so decent because Laura Meister was dying.

'That's silly. She wouldn't go to school if she was dying.'

'Perhaps she doesn't know?'

'If she were dying, she'd be in bed,' Patience decided.

Rose had wistfully been planning Laura's funeral. 'Oh, Patti, you're so *sensible* sometimes.'

Still, Patience did feel anxious for the new girl: that she was lonely, that she was peculiar, that she might not fit in. Then one day in English, when Miss Lowrie was giving her all to Keats who had died so dreadfully young and no one but Rose Delane was listening, a small pale blue envelope arrived on Patience's desk. *Miss Patience Mackenzie* the envelope read and the writing was odd somehow, though careful: spiky as if written with a crossed nib; and the envelope smelled faintly of the kind of scented Christmas soap one puts in drawers with cardigans.

'Laura Meister, what is the first thing we do when the fire-bell rings?' Miss Mallard, who took Games, was also in charge of air-raid practice. She blew her whistle at Laura Meister. Short and breastless, a hockey demon she was, with time only for life's forwards.

'We go to the shelter, ma'am.'

'My name is Mallard, Meister. Miss Mallard. What is my name?'

'Miss Mallard, ma'am.'

'And what do we do before we go to the shelter?'

The whole of the middle school was lined up before the shelter. Snow fell on the sandbags. Posy Potter rubbed her chilblains, one foot against the other. The trees in the Arboretum were bare. Rose Delane sneezed: she had still not got over Keats. A bomb could have fallen and wiped them all out.

'Barbara Baxter, what do we do before we go to the shelter?'

'We get our gas-masks from the cloakroom, Miss Mallard.'

Barbara Baxter, needless to say, was a centre forward. And Laura Meister had no gas-mask. It was possible that she did not know what a gas-mask was, that she came from haunts of coot and hern or faery lands forlorn.

Being a foreigner, she was susceptible to chills.

Patience read the letter the first private moment she had.

Dear Patience,

We would be very glad if you would like to come for tea on Tuesday.

With best wishes,

Laura

This time, Patience excused herself five minutes before the end of the last class, hid in the lavatory until the bell went and caught up with the new girl just as she was leaving the school. Laura walked a little hunched, like a bird with its wings folded. She still had no uniform coat but wore something in a smooth, black material that had probably once been good, with a fur collar turned up, as though she had a grey squirrel round her neck. She looked tired and pinched and her fur hat was brushed with snow, her mittens hand-knitted and lumpy, but as Patience remembered always, for years after whenever she thought of her, there was something exotic about Laura: she had the air of a temporarily disinherited princess, obliged for the moment to travel incognito.

'Thank you very much for your letter,' said Patience. 'I'd like to come on Tuesday. I say, I'm sorry La Mallard was such a pig.'

16

'Well, you see,' Laura said, 'I have no gas-mask. So I suppose I shall have to get one?' She smiled, quite wickedly, and suddenly seemed a different person. Then the light went from her face and she shivered. It was cold and would soon be dark. The snow had turned to a thin, spiteful drizzle. The two girls walked between the Edwardian villas where, behind the blackout, people would be making tea and drawing up their chairs to the fire, complaining comfortably about the weather. It seemed to Patience that here, on this eminence above the town, she was stranded with Laura Meister on some wolf-threatened hillside in winter, with no place to hide.

Then they came to the parting of the ways, the tram stop. Laura walked home – she lived, Patience gathered, in one of those old-fashioned dumps in the Park, which wasn't a park at all, but a lot of big houses that had once been grand and gone down: just like Albert Lodge.

Patience had a peculiar feeling she ought to shake hands, she felt awkward about saying goodbye to Laura, then the tram came swinging round the corner and she could wave and call out: 'If you like, I'll help you get a gas-mask on Monday.'

Laura answered, but she didn't catch her words. As the tram clanged off, Patience pressed her face to the window, but her own breath steamed the glass, and darkness swallowed Laura Meister.

As it happened, both gas-masks and tea parties were put in abeyance. The new girl had fallen ill the day after the air-raid practice and for the fortnight Laura Meister was away Patience nearly forgot her. Except that there was something very *present* about her absence. Her desk insisted on its emptiness. People stopped talking about her and things were almost back to normal but not quite: the crowd seemed to scrap among themselves more than usual and Nina Cherry shaved her legs with her brother's cut-throat and drew blood. One day Patience took the alternative route home – a walk through the Park then a bus from Channing Circus. The afternoons were lighter now and blackout was not necessary before five or six.

It was, as might have been expected, just like any other house in the Park: dusty laurels, flaking paint and grey front garden. Castellated. Spires and turrets, aspirations. Disappointed shrubs, and a smoky cat

17

with quivering tail spat when Patience tried to touch it. She looked up and saw a lamp shining in the topmost turret. Then she ran down the hill, she ran, enchanted and pursued, home to Spring Gardens where the pavements shone, sensible dogs walked about and hedges were privet, gold or green.

2

Beside the door an assortment of bell-pushes and slots containing cards, some clean, some grubby. *Meister*, neatly written in a gothic script with a thin nib and black ink, *flat 3*. Stained glass of St. George with dragon rampant and Una delightfully couchante on green bank with flowers, awaiting the attentions of Rossetti? Or Burne-Jones? At the time, Patience simply saw it and was bewitched. Even now she remembers every detail: the daisies and lilies, the rabbit at Una's feet, the bird in the tree, the languorous maiden attending dreamily the outcome of the battle.

Open the door and follow Laura through the hall and up the stairs. They came in from the sun and the deep shades of the hall were for the moment blinding, so Patience stumbled on the marble floor and reached, to catch her balance, for the heavy, ugly banister. The stairs were uncarpeted, she followed Laura up the stairs and heard below a door open and shut, there was a smell of vegetables overcooked and a filtered light; a house occupied and unregarded.

'Maman?'

A strange room. Curtains drawn, lamplit, queer smell of something heavy and cloying, sickroom and scent; like a cave in which little objects glowed and winked: a toad with a jewel in his head would not have been a surprise. Two deep armchairs and a sofa, stools, a ruby-encrusted egg; photographs – so many photographs in silver or velvet frames; and rugs on the floor and on the walls, actually hanging on the walls. Probably priceless. Then, from a flutter of scarves and heaped, embroidered shawls, and little cushions, Sophy Meister stirred.

'Ah,' breathed Laura's mother, 'so this is Patience – Laura's good friend.'

'Have you a migraine, Maman?'

'Just a little bit, my darling. But go' – said this alarming invalid – 'growing girls must eat, I know that. Go and make yourself sand-wiches! Great sides of bread and jam! Laura doesn't eat enough, Patience. You must see that she eats.'

The kitchen was cosy and ordinary. A wooden table covered in American cloth; pretty plates on the dresser, big ticking clock. While Laura buttered, Patience spread jam. The kettle hummed on the range. Patience said: 'Is your mother an actress?'

Laura poured the tea and sat down, and suddenly she seemed quite ordinary, rather tired. She bit her lip as though trying to make up her mind, then spoke.

'No, she's part Russian, you see, and part French, and English, and so we speak French sometimes. It used to be very smart to speak French in Russia. But of course I had an English governess – my mother insisted.'

'Did you like that?'

'Well, I suppose I thought everyone lived that way – it just seemed normal.' Since she'd drunk her tea, the colour had come back to Laura's face – or, at least, she no longer looked quite so sallow. She smiled for the first time since they had come into the house. 'So, you see, that's why I came to school wearing those awful clothes.'

'I think the uniform's pretty awful too,' Patience said, then pon-dered. 'School's deadly, I know, but I don't think I'd have liked a governess. Was yours nice?'

'One was. When we moved to Paris she was supposed to take me for a walk in the Jardins de Luxembourg every afternoon, but some-times we went to the cinema. Then we'd go back home and I would say: "Yes, Maman, the band was playing in the gardens." I liked Paris better than Berlin, but I think I'll like school better.' Wistfully, Laura added: 'If they'll like me. Miss Trott is very nice, isn't she?'

Patience was staggered at the idea that any of Them – especially Trotty – could actually be described as nice. A few silly girls like Rose Delane had pashes on one or another of the staff but niceness somehow never came into it. It was Us and Them: that was simply the order of things.

Laura washed up and Patience wiped, then they went to Laura's little room in the tower, hardly large enough for a pair of mice, but very pretty, like a room in a story. Laura showed her the locket and snapped it open. Inside there was a portrait of a solemn young man with a stiff collar and short hair.

'That's my brother, Heini,' she said, and smiled openly. 'He's so good looking don't you think? All the girls had crushes on him. Do you have a crush on anyone, Patience?'

'No, not really. I think I'm too young. But Nina Cherry has – or rather, they have on her. She meets boys in the Arboretum.'

'Isn't that against the rules?'

'Oh yes, but she doesn't care.'

'These rules' – Laura reflected. 'I find them difficult because I don't know what they are and I am afraid of breaking them. Are they written down so that I could read them?'

'No. You just have to learn them. I'll help you, if you like. Anyhow, a lot of them are rather silly.'

'Scotty – my governess in Paris – used to say rules were made to be broken.' Laura sat up very straight, as though she had a board down her back; and there was, incarnate, a lapsed Presbyterian Scottish governess with anarchist tendencies, striding past the Luxembourg Gardens on the way to the forbidden cinema. '"Laura," she used to say, "the only way to test rules is to break them. I do not approve of revolution because it is untidy, but we shall go to the pictures."'

'What happened to your brother?' The locket still lay open on the bed, between the girls. He was, indeed, very handsome. Patti hoped he wasn't dead.

Nothing had changed, but Laura had put on that sallow face again, the one she wore at school.

'Heini was in the *Jungvolk*,' she said. 'Then the Hitler Youth and all that. We don't talk about him. I loved him more than anyone in the world and he betrayed my father. It wasn't his fault. That was the rule.' She was sitting on the bed, the locket on her lap, and dipped her face. 'I miss him very much. So does my mother, I think really – that's why she's ill.'

'But that's terrible!' said Patience. 'You mean he's fighting for the Germans?'

'Yes. But then we are German, you see. Little bits of Russian and French and Austrian – there was even an English great-grandmother. That's where I got my name, though when I was born it was very chic anyway to use English names. But we're still German.' Her face brightened. 'One day, if you like, I'll show you the tree. It's quite interesting.'

'The tree?'

'The family tree – who was related to whom and what children they had. My mother and I made it, just like a real tree, with branches and roots. She keeps it locked up but when it's a good day, I'll ask her. What would you like to do now?'

'I think it's time I went home. My mother worries when I'm out in the blackout.'

Just as they reached the foot of the stairs, a door above opened and a man's voice called: 'Laura?'

'Papa? I'm sorry, Patience, but I must go. You will forgive me? That is my father.'

'Of course.' And before Patti could thank her new friend, or say more, Laura had whirled away up the stairs. Her cheeks were positively pink and as Patience pulled on her coat she heard the sound of laughter from upstairs.

All the way home in the tram Patience hugged to herself her strange afternoon. Visiting the Meisters for the first time had been like listening to a story, a melodrama of which some crucial parts remained to be related. The few occasions Patience had been to the Theatre Royal were rather like this: enchanting but frustrating – if the actors were good enough she believed in them so entirely she wanted to follow them offstage as though they could actually lead her into another world that might be dangerous but would certainly prove richer than her own. It was going to be complicated being Laura's friend, she grasped that. The values of school and her peers she had never questioned seriously. Now she might have to take sides, or at least, to dissemble.

. . .

As an establishment for girls, the school was naturally a violent institution. Little girls drew blood, that was actually normal, they fought, they punched and pinched; but because they were supposed to be growing up to be young ladies, there was a conspiracy – it was understood that nothing at all went on.

So Laura Meister was not persecuted. Nor was her lip cut nor did Barbara Baxter run a protection gang. Officially. As far as the authorities were concerned. Beneath the city – under Albert Lodge itself – tunnels carried an underground stream. Everyone knew it was there but hardly anyone ever thought of it.

Spring had arrived at last though this year it was not flowers that bloomed, stiff as soldiers in the Arboretum beds, but vegetables and trenches. A few forgotten crocus pushed through between the feathery carrot tops and early cabbage. The urns crowning the balustrade that gave onto the Arboretum overflowed with a tangle of wild violets the winter had failed to kill and old Bill decided to let live. The air was sharp, bright and nearly warm and the girls were a little mad without knowing why – frets and instincts surfaced that had lain dormant all winter. Nina Cherry spent every free moment with her swains in the Arboretum, Rose Delane was in love with Miss Lowrie and Barbara Baxter flung a tennis ball at Laura Meister, cutting her lip.

Patience found Laura in the subterranean cloakroom, staunching the flow of bright blood with cold water and a towel.

Patience felt helpless. It was cold and dark here, like going back into winter. She had run after Laura, so full of good intentions, but now she could not think what to do or say.

'It was Barbara's fault. I saw.'

'It doesn't matter.'

'Perhaps you ought to have stitches.'

'Look. It's stopped!'

'Your lip's terribly swollen.'

'I'll say I fell over.'

'For many years,' said Miss Trott, flinging open the windows, 'the Dark Ages continued.' She turned to the blackboard and wrote, the chalk grating like rhubarb on your teeth: *Burn now your candle as long as ye will: it has naught to do with me, for my light cometh when the day breaketh*. 'Bede,' she announced, 'the great Bede. Who knew more than you or I.' The bell went but no one moved. Miss Trott walked again to the window where daffodils sang in Posy's jar, rubbed her forefinger along the dusty sill and concluded: 'Tomorrow we shall discuss the role of the Church in the Dark Ages. Nina, will you put away your handkerchief in your sleeve if you have no pocket, and collect the dinner tickets. Laura, do you have some trouble with your mouth?'

The sun continued to shine, sparking motes of dust in the air to gold, striping desks and blackboards. An early bee tumbled in through the open window, buzzed the class and collapsed on Trotty's desk, but if it had been a Heinkel no one would have stirred a whisker: all, in varying attitudes of tension, were awaiting Armageddon and no one dared look at either Laura or Barbara.

Then Laura said: 'I fell down the playground steps, Miss Trott.'

It was as though they had been holding their breath. Then Trotty nodded curtly and left the room. The class could not wait to get out into the sun. No one spoke of the incident. Patience hesitated and thought of going after Laura and was shamed. But the others, the moment school was done, dashed into the Arboretum and she followed them.

Away from the paths and the mothers and prams, trenches and vegetables, notices and shaved grass, was the wild part of the Arboretum, known to the girls, where a kind of maquis flourished (not unlike the boiler-room, though here the park-keeper, rather than old Bill, was the danger). Among the rhododendrons, from April to October, assignations were kept with the High School boys and Nina Cherry sometimes unbuttoned, allowed selected followers to view her breasts; one great day when the earth was warm and the light danced, she even permitted touch and was startled, thrown temporarily off balance by her own delight.

There were laurels too, dusty and somehow sad shrubs. And here, one Thursday half-day, the usual crowd drank Tizer and ate doughnuts from the tuck shop. Patience dozed, watching a beetle climb a twig, and heard Barbara say: 'Well, anyhow, Laura Meister's a Hun. And Patti's got a pash on her.'

Patience knew she was supposed to hear. She clenched her fists and shut her eyes. She felt lonelier and angrier than she ever had in her life, and the beetle climbed and tumbled and climbed, and she lay there long after the earth had cooled and the others had gone. By the time she left, it was almost dark.

Another time, they were in the biology lab at the top of the building listening to a recording Miss Lowrie had borrowed from a real poet of T. S. Eliot reading *The Waste Land*. Perhaps it was the gramophone or the quality of the record but the great man sounded like some paper-eating insect, masticating. *And the dead tree gives no shelter, the cricket no relief/And the dry stone no sound of water.*
There was also the smell of killing fluid, antiseptic death, and an impaled moth. It was hot again so the windows were open and as a counterpoint to Mr Eliot's desiccated rasp there rose from the Arboretum the sound of sawing and hammering. Miss Lowrie waved her watery hands and her acolyte, Rose Delane, closed the windows.
Though she was hopeless, Posy Potter sometimes knew things. It may have been nature compensating her for her disabilities, tuning her in on the ether to signals from elsewhere, but Posy knew, for instance, that it was a camp being built in the Arboretum.
'But a camp what for?'
'Well, prisoners,' said Posy, appalled to be the centre of attention. 'Prisoners of war.'

Through the days that followed, they saw the camp rise: wooden huts and a watchtower, then the fence, seven feet high; it was electro-cuted, Posy said – she meant electrified.
After the first small sensation, the girls hardly regarded the camp: it was though it had always been there. And its purpose – no one thought much about that, either, or no one spoke of it.
Patience made herself look, really look, and thought: they are going to put men in there. She tried to imagine it – men walking up and down in a cage. Their heads would be shaved. If one flung himself against the wire, he would be broken, like a bird in a room. But though she saw it, she could not feel it: it was like a picture.
'*Servus*', said Miss Trott. '*Miser*. The slave is often unhappy

because he is not free. Rose, perhaps you would be good enough to share with us the book you are concealing upon your lap?'

Pretty dotty dreamy Rose, pink as her own name, surrendered Rupert Brooke wrapped in violet tissue, slightly scented. Miss Trott received the offering with distaste.

'Where did you come by this, Rose Delane?'

'Miss Lowrie lent it to me. It's very sad – he died young, like Keats.'

'Indeed. Well, we shall see about that. Some of you girls are morbid, it will be your age. You will learn that death does not automatically bestow grace upon minor poets. Meanwhile, if we are ever to rise to Caesar and Virgil you will transcribe for me, Rose Delane, the imperative passive of *Juliana*: Seek terms of peace, citizens, and appease the Romans with gifts. Be advised by me; send that slave of yours home. Ten thousand enemies are marching through the midst of the land.'

'But they've got to catch them first,' said Nina.

'Who?'

'The prisoners. To put them in the camp.' Nina and Patience were looking for botanical specimens in the Arboretum: they were supposed to take them back and press them for Nature Study but in this ordered park wild life survived only in the maquis, so there they sat, among the rhododendrons, the dusty leaves and the shining webs that by afternoon were always mysteriously gone. Nina smoked – rather well, Patience considered – yawned, then brightened. 'I suppose they might get out and rape us. They're coming disguised as nuns, you know, on parachutes. You can tell by the boots. It's something to do with the Fifth Column. I say, is Laura Meister really a German?'

Patience thought and then she did answer, because, of the crowd, she realised she liked Nina best. She was silly sometimes but daring too, and never, in the years she knew her, now or since, had Nina ever shown malice.

'Only partly. She's English too. And she speaks French best.'

'I think she's rather glamorous. Well, she could be if she got her hair done. They won't put her in the camp, will they? For being German?'

Patience sat up straight, horrified. 'Oh no! They couldn't do that. She's a refugee!'

Something had happened in France and Miss Winterton, the head-mistress, led them in prayer, but that was distant, that was a dream, weather in another country while here, in hall, in school, the world was as it had ever been in summer term. Outside, the bright calling day: places to run and hide and whisper and swim, hoses dancing in Spring Gardens and fat bumble-bees staggering among the first pollen in Mrs Mackenzie's garden. Black secret pools, mild sky and a scent of country that reached, at this time of year, even into the town. For they were mowing the forbidden grass in the Arboretum.

'For those safely returned from across the sea, and those who remain, and those who will never return, may God's grace be upon them.'

'Amen.'

Three hundred girls in their summer dresses – of checked cotton, green, pink or blue – squinted through their fingers, mumbled their amens, raised their bowed heads and went thankfully into the hymn of the day that concluded prayers.

God moves in a mysterious way/His wonders to perform.

The staff were raised on the stage, upon an eminence above the girls. Miss Lowrie had a small, faint voice for hymns and Miss Mallard belted them out like a soldier.

He plants His footsteps in the sea/And rides upon the storm.

And above them all, by virtue of the authority vested in her and the fact that she was very tall and very thin and very just, Miss Winterton, the Head, looked down upon her girls, saw flowers in a field, wondered about a cutlet for supper.

Blind unbelief is sure to err/And scan His work in vain.

Sometimes, the Head felt, there was too great a distance between herself and her charges. All those faces like flowers, and never a chance to explain. The price of absolute power. Even if she could have, the sun was in her eyes, she had no answer. Ham perhaps? And a lettuce? Give me a reason, Oh Lord, if I could believe.

God is His own interpreter/And He will make it plain.

Amen.

·   ·   ·

27

Laura's father, Herr Doktor Meister, took Patience and his daughter out for tea at Fowler and Freebond: a department store whose top-floor restaurant looked out over the city square to the castle. Here, among the potted ferns, a small orchestra still played for the thé dansant.

He was not what she expected. He was a small, neat, dapper man, with a soft moustache like a mouse. Small hands and feet to match, Patience noticed when she took a turn with him round the tiny dance floor.

And yet he did belong to that wonderful, mysterious household: she could see him fetching shawls for Sophy Meister and loving Laura. So that in his presence Laura looked as though someone had told her she was beautiful – as she was when she spoke of her brother, or talked about Paris and playing truant with Scotty.

They had come straight from school, so still wore their uniform gingham, but Laura had twisted her dry, frizzy brown hair up into a knot on top of her head and Patience saw that Nina Cherry was right – Laura could be glamorous.

Patience did not remember very much of what they talked about. There was the scratchy music, and it was someone's birthday. Laura's?

Laura's father said he was not a real doctor: that is, he did not cure people. Quite the opposite – he was a doctor of ideas, and ideas, he said, could be dangerous. Patience was impressed, but even more impressed that he seemed to be able to talk and foxtrot at once.

'Dangerous?'

The foxtrot came to an end, but Doktor Meister detained Patience for a moment on the floor. 'You have been a good friend to my daughter,' he said, 'Laura tells me that. If she should have trouble, I would be happy to know that you were helping her. That would console me.'

'You mean her asthma?'

'And other things. Troubles she might have.'

Patience knew about Laura's asthma. That was why she had been away from school soon after she arrived. Patience discovered because one day – it must have been soon after the camp began to go up – she

28

found Laura dying in the cloakroom when everyone else had gone home. Patience was blackboard monitor that day, so she too was delayed. And there, when she went down to fetch her gas-mask, was Laura rasping for breath. So Laura Meister had to carry tablets with her all the time and she was excused hockey. Anyhow, she remarked once to Patience, Scotty always said that hockey was not chic.

'It's all right. I'm not going to die. And I can play tennis. Scotty taught me.'

Patience's father was somewhere, training it was believed, after that nonsense in Norway. Mrs Mackenzie turned in her bed and dreamed that he came home, walked up the path and through the door and sat down at the table, but he had no face; another time his hands were bleeding. Mary Mackenzie knelt among her lettuce. She was a thin woman with hair that could be pretty. Patience was like her father: big-boned and sandy.

'You could bring your new friend home for tea?'

'I'm not sure. Her mother's not very well. It's a long way.'

'You can.'

'Yes, I know.' Patience stood in the path. She didn't like to see her mother like this: tired and kneeling, as if she were praying for something. She went over to Nina Cherry's on her bike and they tried on make-up and read film magazines.

Then it was really summer and time for the middle-school annual exams. They sat at desks in the gym, supervised on a shift basis by Trotty, Miss Lowrie and Mam'selle – who wore a wig and complained of *les courants d'air*. Miss Lowrie, on the other hand, found the heat vaporous and opened the windows Mademoiselle had shut. Just as well – Posy Potter was looking yellow and Nina Cherry had the curse. That made the torture worse though – the voices of summer outside, the scented air, the racket in the playground at break and the bells rung to mark the periods in the other, the real world. For if the girls found the everyday life of school restricting, from the examination room it seemed wonderfully free.

Les champs d'Angleterre sont beaux, Patience wrote and she pushed back her hair and yawned. Summer always brought out freckles not only on her face, but her arms and legs (Nina Cherry said

29

lemon, but you couldn't get lemons any more, there might not be lemons ever again). She felt large and hot and, looking at the nape of Laura's neck at the desk in front, wished she were pretty like Nina or thin like Laura. Oh, to have what Miss Lowrie called an air and to dance on slim legs and admired ankles; and to be given flowers and bury your face and dance away! (Nina's swain gave her a carnation and she wore it secretly in her bra.) *Les jeunes filles d'Angleterre sont belles* – I shall never have flowers, Patience thought; carnations, violets, roses she saw, and for Laura a single, yellow-white lily like the one Una had in the Meisters' stained-glass door. I shall never have an air.

Laura has an air.

Les jeunes filles de la France aiment les fleurs.

On the last day of the exams Mademoiselle came in late wearing her wig crooked. She looked ill and her eyes were puffy as though she had been crying. She stayed only half an hour and was relieved early. Afterwards, with the last paper handed in, the girls gathered in the corridor outside the gym.

'What was up with her?' Barbara Baxter knew most things – that was partly why you had to keep on the right side of her – but this time her grapevine had let her down.

Patience shook her head. Finally, it was Laura Meister who told them.

'The Germans have entered Paris,' she said. 'That means that France has fallen.'

'Oh,' said Nina, 'I thought someone must be dead.' And the girls ran out into the sunshine.

A week later Laura was called out of class and did not come back. This was a drama that would be much discussed, though not in Trotty's class (she had ears all round her head). Then as the rest were leaving, she called Patience to wait. Before speaking, she wiped the board and sat at her desk, arranging pens and paper as though it mattered that they should be arranged. Patience waited.

'I believe you are a friend of Laura's,' said Miss Trott at last.

'Yes, Miss Trott.'

'Then I think you should know that her father has been arrested.'

And the birds went on singing. It was a lovely day.

3

Democratic though it appeared, the school was an autocracy. Necessarily so for – as Miss Trott pointed out to Miss Winterton more than once – however else would one control three hundred girls, many pubescent?

'For their own good, Head,' said Miss Trott firmly, as the two women looked down from the study on to the playground. 'Anything else would be chaos.'

'Of course, Lucy. You are so sensible.'

They might take another coffee and discuss the principles of benevolent dictatorship. Under the last regime, recalled by Lucy Trott, the school had gone downhill. The improvement since Claire Winterton's arrival was proof of the pudding. The children needed to know where they were – all the more so in present circumstances. Dry though she might appear, Lucy Trott, as a classicist, was romantic in respect of order. For this reason she felt more at home among the Latii of northern Italy than in the south. These were the true descendants of the Romans; debased, of course, in both language and culture, but travelling with Claire two summers ago she had felt quite ill in Naples. Then, 'Greece?' Claire said. Lucy removed the cold compress from her forehead, they ran down the shining sea, down the hill of water into the violet shades of the islands, between the walls of the Corinth canal. And they were standing in Athens before the Parthenon in the clear light of reason.

Oh, that light! It saw through everything, felt Lucy Trott, and Claire too was enraptured: really, the Head looked very splendid in Greece. They fixed their gaze above the picturesque and the squalid (those cheap souvenirs; and those poor cats in the agora and in Hadrian's library – one had to harden one's heart). They looked up and preferred the Erechtheion – the precinct to Athena, she who would stand no nonsense. And they saw the calm, sane lines of the whole Acropolis, still so uncompromising, so certain against the white midday sky.

In the evening they sat in the courtyard of the hotel, by the fig-tree. A lamp was brought out and sometimes they read.

Both were a little in love with Pericles. Think of it! Thirty years of order at the centre of the civilised world! Lucy suspected it was Pericles the good committee chairman, rather than the democrat, who had carried through his vision; and that business of the Ionian confederacy funds appropriated from Delos to Athens – well, did not the end justify the means? Almost every commanding figure in history has had a high-handed streak.

Resignedly, the Head and Miss Trott returned to the end-of-year reports: a burdensome job that surely justified a spot of Claire's rather middling sherry, followed by a peppermint.

'Mallard seems worried about Laura Meister,' said Miss Winterton.

'For what reason? It can't be easy for the poor girl, of course, but that sensible Patience Mackenzie has taken her under her wing. Her French paper was excellent. Naturally. She's tri-lingual.' Lucy Trott took off her spectacles and pinched the bridge of her nose; she felt a prickle of hay fever in her nasal passages and wished dear Claire's study did not always resemble a flower-shop. 'I must admit there is something about the girl – she has a certain style. Not Josephine Mallard's type, I can see that.'

'Mallard feels that she might be a disruptive element. That is, she is not the kind of girl we are used to.'

'Disruptive? Ah, yes. Yes, I see that – or I understand what Mallard sees and wish I didn't.' The way Lucy said Mallard – as though piercing some undesirable insect through the spine and pinning it to a board.

'To intervene or not?' murmured Claire Winterton, but the Head was not soft – she had walked up and down the Atlas mountains; she was like the top of a mountain herself: veiled in vagueness but firm enough when you came to it. 'There is the school to think of, you see,

Lucy; that matters more than all of us. I believe that Laura Meister must sink or swim.'

Justice is impartial, Lucy Trott told herself. Remember Pericles!

Patience stood before Una and the lily. She heard the bell ring in some empty and lonely place, so it sounded, far away.

Almost, she gave up. The house seemed dead, closed, and the little garden was drab with midsummer. The thin cat watched her from under a dusty laurel, then at last Patience heard feet on the stairs. She held her breath. She had not wanted to come. Somehow she felt it might be like visiting the dying or the bereaved – she was unsure of a welcome.

Laura had been away from school for three days after she was called out of class. Now she sat at the kitchen table and told Patience: 'Well, you see my father's a C class alien. He hasn't done anything wrong – he's just an alien.'

'But he's against Hitler!'

'That's why he wasn't interned before. Most of the others were – even Jews and some people like him. Now it's everyone under seventy unless they're ill. Though some of them we know are ill and they took them anyway. That's the rule. They keep inventing new rules as they go along.'

Patience couldn't understand why Laura wasn't crying or screaming, how she could be talking so calmly, how anything could be so *unfair*.

'That's terrible! It must be a mistake – that couldn't happen in England. What are you doing about it? Where is he?'

'We don't know. It was all done quickly and secretly, though they were quite polite. There are rumours they're sending them to Canada and places like that. We're lucky – at least we know what's happened to him and we do have some money. Someone we know – a Jew – committed suicide in May when they rounded up the B class. He had very little money, his wife was ill and the rest of his family is still in Poland. He'd been through it all before and then he thought he was free. I suppose he just couldn't face it again. Would you like some tea? We could take it in to my mother. She likes you – you could cheer her up.'

'I expect she's dreadfully upset, isn't she?'

Laura paused with the kettle halfway to the pot. She frowned with concentration and seemed to need time to consider. Then finally she replied.

'My mother has her own way of doing everything.'

Sometimes, at the oddest moments, Laura Meister could be quite dry.

'Oh, it is enerving,' sighed Sophy Meister, 'quite embeasting.' She fluttered her little scarves and smoked an interesting coloured cigarette in a long holder.

Patience felt large and awkward in this extraordinary room as though, if she moved, glass would shatter, she would be trampling icicles of glass, small, precious, dangerous things. The dimness and the richness and the strangeness. She could choke here, as in a dream, but she had been well brought up.

'I'm sorry,' she said, 'about Doktor Meister.'

'You are a dear girl,' said Sophy and she seemed, for a moment, the witch in the gingerbread house, though she was only Laura's mother and must be unhappy without her husband. Patience wondered if she had lost the use of her legs, that she never got off the sofa. Then, going home, she thought that Sophy Meister was the most glamorous person she had ever met. She was dazzled by her, she felt sorry for her, and she did not like her very much.

Ceremonies were important to the school. It seemed sometimes, indeed, to be the other way round: the school existed to serve the ceremonies. Whichever, the rituals were powerful, commanding, and they were all the more meticulously observed, that these were difficult times.

At the end-of-term prizegiving, for instance, followed in summer by a garden party, staff sported their academic gowns and sandwiches were crustless. Mothers wore hats and even a few fathers appeared. Fewer this year than usual. 'Men!' said Nina Cherry and rolled her eyes. The fathers looked as uncomfortable as hussars in a convent until they found Miss Lowrie – who charmed them and flirted and sighed and smiled, wearing her gown slightly off the shoulder and a seaweed dress.

First though, the prizes, dispensed by the cloud-capped Miss Winterton at her loftiest and most benevolent, flanked on the stage in Hall by governors and senior staff.

'First prize in the fourth year for Latin to Patience Mackenzie.'

The Head wore grey – her best colour – and shook your hand as you took the tissue-wrapped book; rather like the Queen, without squeezing. Patience felt pleased, flushed and clumsy. You walked up one side of the stage and down the other.

Rose Delane got second in Art, Barbara Baxter Games, of course, and Posy Potter Needlework – to everyone's surprise. Nina Cherry didn't mind that she got nothing (it all seemed rather childish to her) but she nudged Patience when the moment came they had all been waiting for.

'And for fourth-year French, Laura Meister.'

Patience held her breath but Laura did it very well. She looked pale but rather beautiful, with her hair in a knot on top of her head, just as she had worn it on her birthday. Though no one moved or spoke, it seemed to Patience – as it had the first time Laura appeared in class, that winter day – that the air was charged, shook; nothing would ever be quite the same again. There was something extraordinary about Laura, something beyond her control: as though she carried with her her own light and, even on a sunless day, trailed her own shadow.

Why did Patience not want Laura to meet her mother? She never knew. Perhaps, though not a girl given to fantasies, she had a fantasy of keeping Laura to herself, as though she could elope with her, be her only true friend for ever, protect her. As though she could.

And in this fantasy there was nothing sexual but something sensuous: some odd peppery scent about Laura's skin, the dark smell of her hair.

Sophy Meister was not at the prizegiving. Mary Mackenzie was.

'So this is Laura. Patience has kept you a mystery. You must come and see us in the holidays.'

'Thank you, Mrs Mackenzie.'

'Is your mother here?'

'She's not – well.'

'I'm sorry.'

Patience left them talking. Later, Laura said: 'I like your mother.' Patience was embarrassed but, after all, quite pleased.

To the last meeting in the Arboretum maquis before the holidays everyone brought something: doughnuts, Tizer, treats. They watched the Boys' High School playing cricket on the pitch only a stone's throw from the prison camp, and talked about sex. In the heat the sounds from the cricket were muffled as if heard underwater, the shapes of the runners danced and trembled. Barbara Baxter yawned.

'It's awful. They push something in you. My mother's got diagrams.'

'Oh,' sighed Rose, 'but it must be lovely to be married.'

'But then you have to have babies!' Posy Potter shuddered.

'No, you don't,' said Barbara. 'You can stop that with the French letter or the Dutch cap.'

'Sex is spiffing,' Nina Cherry said. 'Really spiffing. They take you in their arms and they hold you and kiss you and then you lie down, and then –'

Posy screamed. 'There's a wasp on my doughnut!'

There was the heavy midsummer shade and then the sun and the boys. Patience, half-lying, looked up at the grey leaves, then there was a yell from the pitch and the cricket ball landed at Laura's feet. A fair boy burst through the shrubs and was standing on their sacred ground.

'I say, I'm terribly sorry.' He retrieved the ball and ran off.

'Bloody cheek,' said Barbara.

Patience saw Laura shiver and realised why. For one moment it might have been Heini Meister running out of the sun, the boy in the photograph.

It was end of term, time to go, but the girls stayed on until the match finished and the wicket was cleared. As the shadows reached out to finger the pitch and then the camp, leaving only the watch-tower in sunlight, the girls and the trees and shrubs were mingled, confused, they fell silent, an arm became a branch, a face a dim flower, hands tender leaves; their legs drifted into the darkness of roots. Then as the dusk blotted out their brightness, they trailed home.

Laura turned into her street thinking: this is an English pavement, an *English* pavement. That is an English dog like the one in my picture-book when I was small. In the book all the animals talked, the fields were neat and tidy and green, people lived in cottages and were kind to their dogs. My mother is one-eighth English which makes me one-sixteenth, I suppose. We used to talk English at table and French at weekends – my mother always talked French in restaurants and sometimes Heini and I pretended to be English; we behaved very badly, passing loud remarks about the people sitting in the public gardens, how fat they were, how ugly. We had an imaginary English dog. Our nurse once smacked Heini for making me cry when he said Rover was dead, he'd been run over; but Heini was already too big to be smacked – soon after, they sent him to a proper school and then it wasn't the same, ever again.

When Scotty said you are going to England, I half-expected to be travelling into the picture-book. When it came to the point, most of the time I was too busy looking after Maman. The boat train did go through green fields: it had rained all the way from Paris so everything looked drowned, very green with trees like seaweed, the grass was tall, I felt as though we were travelling across the sea-bed. My father had gone ahead, so I was responsible for my mother. It was a tiring journey. There was a castle and some cows grazed by the line – just like the picture-book – then the sun came out. I still believed that nothing bad could happen in England.

Laura ran the last hundred yards, took a deep breath and turned the key in the lock. Sophy was in the kitchen.

'You're so late! Look, I've burned myself. That stupid kettle. Nothing works in this country.' She held out her wrist as though in a court of justice and there was, indeed, a dull purple stain.

Laura fetched cream and a bandage. As she dressed her mother's hand she told herself, I must make myself always calm while Papa is not here, because my mother cannot manage. She did not want to leave Paris because, she said, there were no *coiffeuses* in England, but really I think she was frightened. That is probably the Russian part of her: she always wants to be somewhere else but she makes up reasons for not going; Scotty was marvellous – she had to be quite fierce to make her go and stood on the platform at St. Lazare until the train started to move. I saw her standing there with her umbrella and the further we drew away, the smaller she got. I do wish Scotty had gone home to Edinburgh. I wish I could write to her. I wish.

When Laura had finished the bandaging, and settled her mother in her room, Sophy touched her cheek.

'Oh, my poor darling, this is hard for you. You are only a child. How can you understand this?'

Laura answered her by rote, out of habit: 'It will be all right, Maman, everything will be all right.'

In her room in the tower, Laura opened a drawer and took out the locket. But Heini's photograph looked flat, his voice had gone and his face too was receding, like Scotty's. Would her father go the same way, through the picture? It seemed to Laura – though she did not put the idea into so many words – that there was England: the one in the picture-book, the one they all talked about, pretty England of smiling cottages and sunny rooms; and leading from these rooms – through small doors, like Alice, behind mirrors, through mirrors, there were darkening and narrowing passages to another world, of cellars and secret camps and dawn arrest. And no one standing in the sunshine seemed to know of this other world.

Then a fair boy burst through the shrubs, running out of the sun, and Laura shivered.

4

Whatever Patience had expected of the holidays, it had not been this. Evacuation.

'Probably only for the summer,' her mother said, 'then we'll see.' But for Patience, summer in the country meant only one thing: summer without Laura. It was disaster! It was absurd! Whoever would want to bomb Spring Gardens?

Patience wrote to Laura from the Manifold Valley:

I suppose it's beautiful. The hills are very high. I went swimming yesterday but the river's freezing! The farm's nice, in fact it's very pretty – if only you could see it. My bedroom has rose wallpaper and we have to wash from a jug in a bowl. They killed some poor old pigs yesterday so we went to the market in Leek because they make a terrible screaming noise. I'm reading a lot. I hope your father's all right.

My mother's just come in and she says why don't you come and stay with us! We could have her double room and she could move into mine. Or if you can't stay, then just for a day or a weekend. There's the train or the Manchester bus, and we'd meet you. Please come . . . And she says if you can't leave your mother, then bring her with you, my mother will write a letter if you want her to. *But you must come.*

Never did Patience believe they would come: Laura would not leave her mother, and how could Sophy Meister travel without legs? Patience was depressed. She collected brown eggs and hated the good weather because Laura would not come. She caught the sun and loathed her big bones, freckles, and sandy hair. She grieved – for what precisely she was not sure, unless it were for Laura – while her mother knitted in the evening and each afternoon took her sun-hat, easel, paper and paints, and set up her camp stool by the river, in the farmyard, or once or twice up on the high bluff above the valley, among the sheep-grass and harebells. Mary Mackenzie saw her daughter flopped in the grass, pulling up tufts of grass, her book thrown aside, and wished for Patience that Laura would come; then she became absorbed by a problem of landscape and wondered if, in this greater view of this strange valley of dry stones and its guarding hills, she had taken on too much? Also, she was tempted by the urge not to dilute the violence of vermilion and viridian, to use them unwatered. She held in her mind un-English landscapes she had never visited, white walls stained by tumbling flowers, a haze of mimosa, burnt-sienna earth and urns of burnt sienna spilling violets and trailing geraniums; hedges of hydrangea and fuchsia, from a terrace of vines a glimpse of a sea burned white. She sighed. She laid on her wash.

Sophy Meister had the use of her legs, after all. She stood on the platform, wearing a silk dress and floppy hat and her legs held her. By way of greeting she called: 'But this is so beautiful!' for anyone to hear. Her legs carried her along the road to the farm and here there were yet more raptures. It was a perfect, still day of late summer, of fragile, piercing light, an ochreous sun warming the stone of the cottages, gilding the trees: it seemed a colour one could taste, like honey.

Patience took Laura to see the kittens. Dazzled by the sun, they stood in the barn. The cat watched them as they crouched to look. Now they were alone, Patience felt shy with Laura.

'They're blind when they're born and their eyes are always blue.' It seemed important that Laura should be interested in the kittens.

'You can pick one up – she won't mind. I'm terribly glad you could come.'

'It's lovely here. It's the nicest place I've been in England.'

'Look: this is the prettiest one. She had seven but one died – she wouldn't feed it and they said it would be cruel to keep it alive. I'm glad your mother could come.' (That wasn't true. Patience was not at all glad.)

'I couldn't leave her, you see.'

They sat in the straw. From here they could see the two mothers come out of the door of the farmhouse and walk down the garden path – they seemed to be discussing flowers because Mrs Meister bent to snap off a stalk of lavender. The kitten on Laura's lap opened its mouth in a soundless mew. It smelled of milk.

'We could go blackberrying. If it's not too tiring. But your mother seems much better.'

Laura's head was dipped over the kitten, her expression secret and in shade. Then she said something Patience hardly caught and certainly did not understand.

'*Elle est morphiniste.*'

Sophy Meister's legs took her up the hill with no effort at all, it seemed. She even led the way. When her silly shoes bothered her, she took them off and carried them: she seemed not to care that her stockings would be dirty and torn. Patience found herself liking Mrs Meister a little better, in spite of the stupid dress; it would be hard to dislike anyone who was so obviously enjoying themselves.

Three-quarters of the way up the hill, just below the blackberry bushes, there was a natural shelf of greener, springy grass, and here they laid out the picnic. Sophy flung herself down and pulled off her hat, revealing a tumble of dark hair with a reddish glint. 'I'm so happy,' she said when she had caught her breath, and for once she seemed not to be acting. 'You know, when I was Laura's age we had such wonderful picnics.'

Mary Mackenzie opened the greaseproof-paper parcels and handed round sandwiches. 'This isn't very much, I'm afraid. We cook for ourselves. But at least we can get a chicken sometimes.'

'Chicken!'

The sky was empty and clear. A horse-drawn plough turned in the valley and wisps of smoke from farms and cottages and bonfires rose straight and still. Mrs Mackenzie smoothed the greaseproof paper and put it back in the picnic bag; she screwed up the Thermos tight, glanced up the hill where the girls had gone, and down at the valley, and began to sketch. Sophy Meister sat with her arms round her knees.

There was no breeze, not an air. It was hot. Patience and Laura picked blackberries, working steadily between the bushes, filling the bowl, until they reached the very top of the hill and rested. Patience looked at her hands: they were stained purple and her nails were black.

'Have you heard about your father?' It seemed safe to ask now. Patience lay on her back, with her hands behind her head and looked up at the sky, a small dot forming and hovering: a lark?

'Well, yes, we've heard he's near Birmingham, but we're not allowed to see him, and I think they're censoring letters. It's not very nice: someone said they're in tents without mattresses. But it's worse in Lancashire – they're in factories with rats, and no books, and not much to eat. It's a good thing my mother has a French passport. I don't think she'd manage.'

'Oh, Laura. How terrible.'

The bird fell out of the sky. Not a lark, but a sparrowhawk.

A figure, Sophy Meister, was climbing the hill, picking the blackberries and eating them. Something really dreadful occurred to Patience.

'You are coming back to school next term, aren't you?'

'Oh yes. But won't you still be evacuated?'

'I hadn't thought of that.'

'Scotty would like it here,' said Laura. 'She liked fresh air.' Laura grinned, and stood up, straight as a soldier. 'Miss Patience Mackenzie, we shall take fresh air and exercise.'

'Race you to the bottom!'

'Don't spill the blackberries!'

You could see seven counties from here, Mary Mackenzie understood. Sometimes she felt quite dizzy on these hills; when she looked up suddenly they toppled and the sky dipped. From this vantage the weather advanced from a great distance and she could see now, from a dangerous clarity on the far horizon, that tomorrow it would rain. It was in small things she most missed Graham: no one to turn to to say, it will rain tomorrow. Well, Patience, of course, but she was too young to understand the consolation of trivia. It must be worse, in a way, for Laura's mother, though at least in the camp her husband would surely survive? An odd woman, rather tiring, but interesting, like a weird, wonderful and damaged bird that had flown in at the window. A little of her would probably be enough. Though Mary was sorry for her: she was the kind of woman who would manage badly without a man.

Sophy was caught in a mesh of brambles: the girls had to release her. Her silk dress was snagged and stained, her hair wild. 'What a fright I am!' She didn't care, she was laughing. She caught the girls by the hands, one on each side, and ran down the hill with them. Patience thought, she is running because she is frightened of something, she is afraid to keep still.

Back at the farm they had boiled eggs (eggs!) at a little table in the front parlour that was the Mackenzies' sitting-room. There was a golden fish in a bowl on the deep window-sill, and Crown Derby in a locked, glass-fronted cupboard. Unread books with drab covers, hard wing-chairs never used and an empty grate – but all transformed by a light like amber resin. While Sophy repaired herself for the train, Patience took Laura up to her room. The day was suddenly slipping away too fast: she felt she had shown her nothing, nothing that really mattered had been said.

'I do wish you could stay!'

'So do I.'

'Look, you can see the orchard from here. The apples aren't ready, but the plums are lovely.' There they were, two girls in a high, small window, above an orchard that smelled of cider, looking down through the ceiling of branches at the fruit that hung very still and was polished by the light, soaked in green-gold by the light – the colour you get in England sometimes that means fruition and decay. Then the wasps burrow in the bird-pecked fruit; and the landscape, even a small orchard, takes on the tense stillness of a stage: but there is no drama, nothing happens, except that the two mothers are walking between the trees and laughing. Have they become friends? The trees are heavy, burdened, they accept. They have no choice. You have to step carefully, for wasps among the fallen fruit. Watching their mothers, the two girls touch, their heads touch, one fair, one dark.

'I'm sure your father will be all right.'

'I expect so.'

'I can't imagine not going back to school, can you? I mean, I hate it sometimes, but I'd miss everyone. Well, Nina and you, and Rose is a bit silly but she can't help it.'

'My father says the war will be over in a year.'

'Who'll win?'

'He doesn't say, but I think he believes Germany will. That would be awful. They make slaves of the people they conquer and take them back to Germany.'

'I wonder if we'll get Trotty again next term. I think we'll come back. I think my mother wants to go home.'

'I'm a bit afraid to go back to school,' Laura confessed. 'I don't know why, when almost everyone's so nice to me.'

'It's funny about school. You want to go and yet you don't, and it's silly even to think about it: you have no choice anyway. I don't mind it really, but I get sick sometimes of being told what to do.'

'It's been a lovely day, Patience.'

Then it was time to go. The light drained from the orchard and the mothers were strolling in sad pools of shade; Sophy Meister pulled her shawl around her and Mary Mackenzie turned, to go back to the house. She called up to the girls: 'Time to go'; then the stage was empty. An apple fell, and at once the drunken wasps clustered around it.

5

'The most *fantas*-tic news,' said Nina Cherry. 'The divine Lowrie's fixed it! We're having this year's play with the Boys' High!'

Barbara Baxter snorted, but Rose Delane was impressed.

'They'd never let us.'

'Well they are.'

'Who said so?'

'Never mind.'

'Shut up. Here's Trotty.'

'Milk monitor this term will be Posy Potter,' said Miss Trott, 'who will also collect dinner tickets. Do you suppose you can manage that, Posy? Good. New prefects are Patience Mackenzie and Barbara Baxter. Badges will be handed out as usual at morning prayers. I can only hope that you will both live up to your awesome responsibility. Remember that power is not a privilege but a burden. There is nothing wrong with it at all, provided it is properly used.'

Patience and her mother were not the only ones to return that autumn from an evacuation that seemed now as remote as the summer: a queer interval out of time, out of war, out of living, somehow. It was instinctive, this return, unreasoned, not a matter of courage or foolhardiness; people just went home, dogs were walked again in Spring Gardens, Germans did not arrive on parachutes, disguised as nuns. At Matlock Spa, that summer, Claire Winterton had raised with Lucy Trott the possibility of evacuating the school. She had a vague idea of alfresco lessons in some country Eden, but Lucy was right, of course. A brisk walk up the Heights of Abraham put everything in perspective.

The life of the school was organic. For a while, at the beginning of the new term, with fresh timetables, unfamiliar faces, holidays remembered and recounted, the girls in their winter tunics or skirts and Viyella shirts were momentarily bemused between two worlds – some bore the stains of tears before a skipped breakfast, others were noisier than usual, there was a little hysteria; competition for the best desk, the prized coat-peg, the eye of the teacher. As in any closed society, as among recidivists in prison or the blessed in heaven themselves, as in all organic matter, cells were powerfully driven to rearrange themselves. New loyalties were considered and often formed, last year's crush sometimes regretted.

Lord behold us with Thy blessing/Once again assembled here

Not unlike the arrangement of the universe, thought Lucy Trott as she surveyed the newly gathered school. Claire and her archangels raised above; a little below, the sixth form, and in the well of the hall the field of folk that made up common humanity. And in time, in the proper order of things, the chosen would be plucked up and take their place among the blessed or two steps down, at least. Of course, there would be those who fell by the way. There would be injustice: something Claire always had difficulty in accepting. But that was perhaps the price of order? Claire herself had said it – the school matters more than all of us.

In the morning we run to school; in the evening we come home, says Julia, and Lucy Trott regrets sometimes that the girls are lost to them every evening, every morning the school must be freshly created. Yet it is so created, each day this miracle takes place. Lucy Trott has one of the small Edwardian villas across the road and at night she will occasionally let herself in and walk the corridors of Albert Lodge, sit for a moment in a classroom, open and close cupboards, doors, desks – not prying, you understand, though what she finds she finds. Rather, as though she were visiting a sleeper's bed, Lucy is testing that the school still breathes; she listens for the thrum of the boiler, the rattle of the pipes, a window bang, a mouse run, a board creak. Sometimes she pulls down the blinds, for the blackout, sometimes she prefers the dark, or by moonlight to patrol the sleeping school.

Keep the spell of home affection/Still alive in every heart.

Well, naturally, thinks Lucy, that is natural. She sighs only faintly and as the morning sun streams blindingly in, her eyes water: hardly has summer hay fever gone than winter sinus strikes. Lowrie has a new dress, she sees – where does she get the coupons? – and her stockings are silk. A rather foolish girl who puts nonsense into the children's heads, though one doubts if anyone but Rose Delane retains it. Lowrie will find some man to protect her and do no harm. Meanwhile, there is the matter of that play with the little boys from down the road – heaven knows what foolishness this will lead to. For once, Lucy cannot rationally back her judgment; she simply regrets this invasion of what seems to her in almost every other aspect an ideal society. A *contained* society. Breach the walls, she fears, and chaos may follow.

Break temptation's fatal power/Shielding all with guardian care,

Yes, we do shield, thinks Claire Winterton, that is our job and our inclination. Her mind strays, it is the singing. How she loves the sweet hymns of her vicarage childhood when Dada was alive. Why did he leave them? When he died, when his gentleness and strength were withdrawn, then God died too. If she could reproduce his kingdom on earth, might he return? And he chastiseth us also – I must be as strong as that, always on guard, I must not think too much of flowers, and the light over Sunion. I am tired. Will the boiler break down this winter? Will there be trouble from that German girl? And the matter of the play: Lucy disapproves, I can see, and girls can be so easily misled. Then we crack down on transgressors! They know that. No compromise! The good of the whole is greater than any one of its parts. I trust my girls and I watch them. Dada, I shall forget those seas and those lights, the fish boiling in the Straits of Salamis, and bear this winter with fortitude. My girls shall be my flowers. With Lucy's help, I shall preserve them from all evil. Claire smiled and brushed from her skirt an invisible crumb of dust.

Safe in every careless hour/Safe from sloth and sensual snare;
Thou, our Saviour/Still our failing strength repair.

'Let us pray.'

·   ·   ·

Patience looked through her fingers at the sixth form ranged just below the staff, and remembered, when she was young, what wonderful, inaccessible creatures they were. Facing the rest of the school and the morning sun, they were bathed in light as a heavenly host and it seemed impossible she would ever be one of them. Everywhere they moved and were encountered, they seemed to carry this light with them and almost all were the object of someone's adoration: though she thought pashes were stupid, she had even been a little in love herself: blushed when she had to pass her heroine in a corridor, trembled when she was addressed, had odd dreams that bothered and exhausted her. But Patience's agonies had been nothing compared to the general mooning and swooning that went on. The worst case was Rose Delane who, until she fell for Miss Lowrie, had a new unrequited passion every week. Flowers, apples, Valentines, tears, servitude and longing: oh, poor Rose! Nina, really, had been the only one quite exempt, but then she got the curse and wore a bra before anyone else and had boy cousins. And Laura. It was hard to imagine that Laura had ever been like that. She seemed to Patience to be both very old and very young. That is, Laura could be hurt, terribly; and at the same time, a part of her belonged to the mysterious adult world, had been claimed already by pains and griefs and possibilities as distant to most of them as a view across an impassable valley.

Now they were in the fifth form, and some of them prefects, the older girls had lost for them most of their glamour. And now too, Patience supposed, they in turn would have their own followers. Several little girls already pursue Barbara because she's the star at hockey. And people will fall in love with Laura – they're sure to. Not me though: I'm not beautiful or sporty, no one will give me flowers or apples or dream of me. It will be the same when I grow up. I don't mind. There are lots of things I can do. People tell me their secrets because they think I'm sensible. Perhaps I'll be able to help Laura? I wish I could help her now. If she were in trouble, if I could rescue her from a burning house.

Trotty passed Miss Winterton the tray of little blue metal badges as if she were serving cucumber sandwiches.

'Barbara Baxter!'

'Patience Mackenzie!'

Miss Winterton smiled vaguely and stepped back as Patience pinned the badge on her tunic. She felt foolish. What was one supposed to do? Salute? No, apparently one shook hands. Miss Winterton's hand was very dry and cool, bony yet insubstantial; then there was at the last moment the very slightest pressure of the thumb on Patience's palm, like a secret code, a message the Head now delivered in tones meant for Patience alone: 'This is a great trust we place in you, Patience my dear; you must pray for the strength to discharge it. You will be a soldier for us, I know. Fight the good fight.'

Then, according to custom, the file of new prefects led the way from the hall while Mademoiselle thumped out the last hymn, her wig bouncing.

Patience found that now she was a prefect, the sixth-form archangels actually took notice of her as though she had suddenly emerged from invisibility. Distantly they took notice, nodding from Parnassus, acknowledging the presence of a new acolyte on the foothills. She would still have to knock at the door of the sixth-form study, of course, was still subject to their discipline, but had climbed, certainly, one rung in the hierarchy, one step towards desired perfection. It all sounded rather like that order of castles, or whatever they were, Laura's brother had to go through before he was allowed to be a soldier. Or an airman, rather. Patience had never dared to ask how Heini had betrayed his father. She dreamed of him once or twice, or the idea of him, flying over England and dropping bombs that did not so much explode as open like flowers and drift down very quietly. And they took root in the earth and grew, then bared their crimson petals. And the flowers were bleeding.

They were sitting in James Fleet's conservatory, sanctum for the fifth and sixth forms. Nina was trying to catch a run in her stockings with nail varnish. Outside the October wind snatched the leaves from the trees and whirled them around; and the children playing caught them and seemed tossed among the leaves, driven themselves to frenzy yet maintaining clearly some kind of pattern of play of their own in spite of the leaves.

Patience watched the play. It seemed no game she could remember. Some kind of ferocious chase, then one would be captured and made to stand in the circle beneath the netball post, while the others marched up and down.

'What are the infants playing?'

'English and Germans.'

If Laura heard, she gave no sign but went on writing, her head bent over her book.

The prison camp in the Arboretum was now complete. Most of the time they hardly noticed it, it had become a certainty of the landscape as unremarked as the maquis among the shrubs, the combed grass, the neat and tended beds, the children's swings and the boys' cricket pitch. Only in the morning mist did the shapes of watchtower and high fence cause anyone to look twice – as they formed, it seemed, from a damp nothingness; and then in the autumn dusk when the same scrawl lost its sharpness and became almost beautiful, as it was wiped away.

One morning it was revealed as shining with hoar-frost: every part, metal or wood, each tendril of barbed wire, glinting and shining with frozen air.

About this time, they first thought they glimpsed figures moving slowly about and plumes of smoke from the huts.

On the same day of the iron frost, the Boys' School OTC made its sensational debut, marching up and down between the terrace of Albert Lodge and the camp, turning and wheeling and stamping, churning their precious pitch.

'What are they doing?' said Posy, leaning out of the window so far, she might have fallen. 'Why are they wearing those uniforms? Are they soldiers?'

'Just pretending.'

Rose Delane was impressed, if she had had flowers she would have thrown them. Trotty was not amused. 'If you can tear yourselves away from the little boys playing soldiers, perhaps we might turn to matters more eternal. And so, as the great Bede had foreseen, the day came, after many years of darkness, when the barbarians laid down their swords and were stilled, and culture flowered once again. Rose, will you please stop sniffing. Barbara, close the windows.'

Something bothered Patience about that day's incident, there was something about it she recognised, though she had hardly seen a soldier in her life. Then she found it, reading with a torch under the bedclothes, the book Miss Lowrie had lent her:

> *Under a grey October sky*
> *The little squads that drill*
> *Click arms and legs mechanically,*
> *Emptied of ragged will! . . .*
> *. . . The rooks from out the tall gaunt trees*
> *In Shrieking circles pass;*
> *Click, clack, click, clack, go Death's trim men*
> *Across the Autumn grass.*

How sad and bitter that seemed, not at all like the other one about dying bravely because you'd pledged your word. Patience suspected that Miss Trott might have approved of this one, better than Rose's Rupert Brooke. Miss Lowrie probably wouldn't like it at all. What was the difference, Patience wondered? Did one tell the truth and the other not? It was puzzling. Words seemed to be so powerful, they could change your feelings from one moment to the next, even words by someone you never knew and who was probably dead. Was that what Laura's father meant when he said ideas were dangerous? Was that what he was being punished for? Words? But if in Germany they had been the wrong words, how could they be the wrong words here too?

Patience turned out the light and stuffed the book under the pillow. She would have to return it some time but she didn't feel at all like discussing it with anyone – especially with Miss Lowrie.

She lay in the dark and was visited by the idea of her father walking towards her. Then click clack he went, one of Death's trim men, and never even smiled.

The first day's high nerves forgotten, the holidays as distant as a story in a book, the girls were generally thankful when the school routine re-established itself. Now it was home that was a little unreal, and going home they felt like soldiers on short leave, torn between two worlds; as for their third world, the war, in spite of the night bombing that had now begun, in spite of the camp, that still seemed a circumstance oddly unrelated to their lives. Partly, they were influenced by Miss Trott's opinion that the less said about that, the better. More, it began to feel as though they had always lived like this: carried gas-masks, been woken at night to sleep in air-raid shelters, or in the coal-house, or under the stairs, gone to school each morning through streets that had been re-arranged overnight by the Luftwaffe – not that it was anything like London: just a corner shop missing, a few fires around the marshalling yard at the station, a near miss at the Castle. 'Gels with backbone,' said La Mallard, 'can get used to anything!' Mademoiselle sniffed. '*On m'a dit*', she confided with brimming eyes, 'that they have buried the Impressionists.'

Laura said that was rather awful. When they were living in Paris, she and Scotty had gone to the Jeu de Paume. Scotty preferred photographs (hence her passion for the cinema?) but there was the most beautiful picture of a girl in white walking through an orchard: even Scotty liked that one and bought a picture postcard. If what Mademoiselle said was true then, of course, it was good – the Nazis would not get the picture. But once, as she closed her eyes in the cellar she and her mother shared with the rest of the house in air-raids, Laura half dreamed of the girl in white, lying under the ground, and dust filled her eyes.

Miss Trott made them transcribe the story of Persephone who was sought by her mother under the earth in Pluto's kingdom. Laura had a fear of being buried: a terrible fear. She thought of the house falling on them, which would be so much worse than dying in the open air. One day, walking to school, she passed a site where men dug furiously. It was a bright, frosty morning. A woman with blackened face and reddened eyes sat among the rubble cradling what appeared to be a baby; then Laura looked more closely and saw that it was a doll. She and her mother knitted socks for seamen, like everyone else. People were polite but Laura had the feeling that they were not welcome in the cellar. Sometimes, they did not go down and while Sophy Meister slept her drugged sleep, Laura would watch from her window. Often nothing would happen at all (the city was not a prime target); then, another time, there would be the most incredible display of pyrotechnics: it was hard to believe that anything so beautiful could be deadly.

It was nothing obvious. No one actually called Laura a Jerry to her face; in a way, it was nothing at all to do with the war. She was different. That might have been enough for them to peck her to death. They were gathering evidence. History is a slow process. And who were they? Miss Mallard, her lieutenant, Barbara Baxter, and some young followers: too modest a caucus to start a pogrom, judged Lucy Trott. Let well alone.

Josephine Mallard put down her foot about hockey. If Laura Meister were to be excused, she must produce a doctor's certificate. Even then she must take air and exercise by walking round the pitch twenty times while the game was in progress.

'Don't you care?' said Patience.

'Oh, no. I used to do a lot of walking with Scotty. They're rather alike, Miss Mallard and Scotty. Except that Scotty made me laugh, and I think she quite liked me. Well, she didn't mind me, anyway.'

'But that was in Paris.'

'Yes. It wasn't so muddy.'

'Are you coming down to the boiler-room at break? Nina's got some chocolate.'

'No, I don't think so.'

'Well, I'll get some for you. Nina's all right.'

Patience was relieved and ashamed. She knew Barbara didn't want Laura in the boiler-room and she was hurt for Laura; and at the same time she would have found it hard to exile herself. So she went, but did not enjoy herself, and that was the worst of both worlds.

November was a busy month. There were the dancing classes and the preparations for the play: both winter sports. Patience always had to lead in the dancing, though she didn't mind so much this year, having Laura for a partner. Laura confessed that sometimes she and Scotty used to dance to the gramophone in the Paris apartment when everyone was out – but not this kind of dancing: Charlestons and tangos; it was a joke really, and often they collapsed laughing. Laura found this extraordinary plodding round of girls with girls rather absurd.

And in November Patience went with Laura and her mother to see Doktor Meister at the camp near Birmingham. It was Sophy who asked, rather as though she were inviting Patience to a picnic or a tennis party.

'Oh, Maman,' Laura said, 'why ever should Patti want to come? It won't be a bit interesting.'

It was one of Sophy's good days. On a wet Saturday afternoon, they were in her boudoir-sitting-room, cosy by the fire with the curtains drawn. It was the wonderful, winking cave again, as Patience had first seen it, but no longer threatening. Welcoming indeed – for Sophy had commanded the fabled family tree to be produced and laughed and made comments, and smoked her pretty coloured cigarettes as, under the fringed and pleated lamp, they studied the tree. And it was truly a tree, drawn with faded Indian ink on thick paper, a tree of trunk and branches and leaves and roots. The leaves and fruit were coloured as though by some good school-child in a nursery years ago. The names perched like birds on the branches, and beneath the roots was even a nest of little mice. For almost every name – at least on the higher branches – Sophy could point to one of the many photographs that cluttered the room.

'Oh! Max and Ferdi!' she cried, 'they had a duel. Ferdi accused Max of cheating in the game book, and there was the most frightful row. But that was the year dot – your father's side. The Germans.' Sophy snatched up a silver-framed photograph from one of many little tables. 'Now *there*,' she said, 'is tante Marie-Louise by the Black Sea.' Patience and Laura inspected a blurred, sepia lady sitting on a chair under an umbrella: she looked like Victoria after Albert. 'Such a beauty!' sighed Sophy, and confided – as though Rasputin might be huddled behind the arras – 'they say the Archduke had his eyes on her. Oh dear, everything did get rather dull after the war. And then those grocers from Odessa – it was never the same after that.'

'What was wrong with them?' asked Laura.

'Well, nothing really, and one shouldn't say it. But *Jews*, you know. But Patience will be bored with our family stories.'

'I think it's very interesting.'

So she did. In fact, Patience was enchanted. She had the same feeling that she had before, only stronger, that visiting the Meisters – just knowing them – was like standing in the wings while on the stage some great drama was enacted she was compelled to witness. Laura, she suspected, did not feel the same, she was very quiet for the rest of the afternoon. She seemed to be watching her mother covertly and anxiously, and appeared almost relieved when it was time for Patience to leave.

In the hall, Patience said: 'I'd like to come to Birmingham with you. If you want me to.'

'Of course I do,' said Laura, a little stiffly. 'Though it won't be much fun.'

And at the door she didn't seem to know what to do, how to take leave, and even stretched out her hand as though she had forgotten the English do not shake hands at parting.

'You mustn't believe everything my mother says.'

She spoke so softly, Patience was not sure she had spoken at all, and all the time Laura seemed to be listening, over her shoulder. She had shut the door before Patience was halfway down the drive.

Mrs Meister (a title she preferred to Frau Doktor, for obvious reasons) wore an old Paris suit that had seen better days though it still had style, and a Robin Hood kind of hat, but in red, not green: it was even shot through with a feather. She attracted attention. By her side, Laura looked like a drab sparrow ('such a pity Laura is so plain' her mother would say, and Laura would pretend not to hear, and hunch her shoulders and fold her wings and look out at the passing landscape).

When Patience remembered that war – for years afterwards, when some small signal tugged at her memory, or she woke in the night, long after it had been folded away and become almost a story – then for some reason the war became always that train journey to and from the outskirts of Birmingham, though it was by no means the most important thing that happened.

55

So the war was a journey taken on a cold November day through unnamed stations, a journey of unexpected changes and unexplained halts between stations in flat country beneath grey skies. Tired soldiers slept or played cards. They were held up for an hour at Nuneaton and a rumour passed down the train that after last night's hit, there was a five-mile cordon round Coventry. In the midday light they saw a pall of darkness, like night, covering the city to the south. A few miles on from Nuneaton, the train slowed again, and they saw a pretty village, a country lane, and a dazed file of people pushing carts and prams, loaded with furniture and bedding and children: they walked as though asleep, a defeated army of somnambulists. Laura noticed that most in their carriage merely glanced and looked quickly away, expressionless, as the British do when they pass a street accident. One man shook his head, but no one spoke until her mother murmured faintly to herself: '*Les pauvres. O les pauvres.*'

Some kind of park. A lodge where their papers were inspected. A wait. They ate the sandwiches Mary Mackenzie had packed. Through a glass partition they could see a guard-room office, soldiers drinking tea. They could not hear their voices, but one spoke and the other laughed. In the waiting-room there were three others – one couple and a woman alone – and they looked quite ordinary. In spite of the small paraffin stove in the corner, it was bitterly cold. From where they sat, the windows were flat grey, pictures of the sky. When Patience stood to look out, the three strangers waiting stirred, they seemed startled, alarmed, then when no threat appeared, they settled again. For a moment Patience felt Laura and her mother to belong to the strangers, herself the odd one out. When she spoke her voice rang too loud, too English in her ears, though she was almost whispering.

'It's quite a pretty park,' she told Laura. 'I mean, there's a lot of grass and a house – I can't see any tents, so perhaps he's in the house?'

Sophy Meister might not have heard. She rested her head against the wall, her eyes closed, as though utterly exhausted. The absurd Robin Hood feather fell over one eye.

The small woman on her own suddenly spoke, addressing no one in particular.

'I am waiting to see my son. My husband was on the *Arandora Star*. They were taking him to Canada and he was torpedoed. We had a nice little restaurant, the Colombino in Charlotte Street.'

Sophy Meister smiled vaguely. The couple also waiting nodded but did not utter, simply moved closer together. They held hands. Perhaps they did not speak English.

Patience wondered how they could be so passive. They all seemed ready to wait forever.

'Oh, my dear loves! And Miss Patience, the foxtrot-dancer!'

Patience smiled as Doktor Meister pressed her hand. She felt shy. She had no place here. They were in a room where two men played ping-pong on a green table. They sat in a window-seat. Outside the tall windows the last leaves were ripped from the trees and the rooks with their ragged, dusty wings, swarming, gathering, swooping, left their empty, giant nests, cried: winter! An elderly man walked through, pushing a trolley, serving tea from an urn. The cups were tin with a blue band round the rim, cracked in places. Sophy shuddered and shook her head; she had repaired her face in the waiting-room when their name was called, and looked almost spry. Her eyes were very bright. Patience had thought that Laura would run into her father's arms but instead she sat there, quite still, almost subdued, holding his hand.

The three were talking now in a mixture of French, German and English, but mostly French. At the far end of the sparsely furnished room Patience noticed a bookcase, and walked over to it. Tolstoy, *Manon Lescaut* in French, Dornford Yates, Sir Walter Scott, Michael Arlen and a Russian dictionary.

At last, she felt a hand on her shoulder.

'Ah,' said Doktor Meister, 'I do enjoy your Dornford Yates. There the rotters always get a ducking. Here it is more complicated, I think?'

'Complicated?'

'You see,' he confided, as though imparting a secret: 'They cannot quite make up their minds which of us here are rotters.' Patience saw how thin his wrist was, as he rested his hand on her arm, and his shirt-cuff was frayed. At least he wasn't in some sort of prison uniform, but his clothes looked as though they had been made for a bigger man, or he had somehow shrunk inside them. She would never normally have noticed a man's hands, but his had been so immaculate and now they were rough, with the nails torn. That shocked her. She was more shocked that the Doktor had observed her. 'You understand' he said, 'we are permitted to grow our own vegetables! I am quite proud of my cabbages. Would you like to see my garden, Miss Patience?'

'Yes, please.'

So they walked in the grounds, inspected cabbages, and Doktor Meister told them the place had once been a school. Then, as is the way with an English November, just towards the end of the afternoon, the dark day was rolled back to reveal the calmest and most beautiful of skies: mild as milk, the softest blue, shot with pink and lemon and gold. The rooks ceased their constant fretting, wheeled once across the sky, were silent. The grass that had seemed so drab, grey as old hair, was fired to an effulgent, acid green. Hanging on her husband's arm, walking ahead of the girls, Sophy Meister had difficulty with her high heels. She leaned towards her husband, then pulled off her silly hat and shook her hair free.

'You see,' said Laura, 'they love each other very much.'

The girls turned and walked back to the house.

Patience said – too brightly, she felt – 'It doesn't seem such a bad place. I mean, it's better than tents. Or being torpedoed.'

They sat on a bench by the wall of the house, overgrown with Virginia creeper. The Meisters had turned and were coming down the slope of grass towards them.

'I can't bear to see him like this,' Laura said.

Patience wanted so much to help her. She longed to touch her and yet she could not. Dare not? What was it? Girls at school walked arm-in-arm, tussled, hugged, she had herself – but with Laura she could not so much as reach out to touch her hand.

Then when Laura smiled, directly at her, for her, as she did now – then Patience felt triumphant as though someone had told her she was beautiful and loved. When her father, the big, sandy, gentle man, embraced her. When she was a child.

58

Laura smiled. 'Thank you for coming,' she said. 'I'm glad you were here. Truly.'

From the moment the woman boarded the train, pushing the child before her into the packed carriage, there had seemed to be something wild, a little mad about her. She had red-rimmed eyes, her face was smudged with soot and the dim blue light hollowed her cheeks. Her fellow-passengers moved up to make room for her in the last seat, and looked away, embarrassed. She clung to a big leather bag on her lap, refused to let go of it even while the child, tired and fretful, tried to clamber up. The child whined. The woman plucked at her back, her coat, she could not keep her hands still.

The soldier beside her – a big-boned man who looked like a farmer – hoisted the infant onto his lap.

'Come on then. Room here for a tuppenny one.' He made the child comfortable. It seemed happy. 'Bad down there, is it love?'

The woman looked dazed for a moment, then this human contact perhaps, or the child being stilled, unlocked her voice. She spoke to the soldier, then turned, looking, her eyes ranging in the carriage, demanding now, shrill with grief and complaint.

'The Cathedral's gone. The city's finished, it's terrible, you should have seen it – people were crying in the streets. Everyone's getting out. It's finished. That Jerry bastard's finished us. London's nothing on that. They don't know what those Jerry bastards can do. No one knows. We're going to his gran's but there's hundreds dead, thousands.' Suddenly her body jerked as though from a blow to the spine, and she was weeping with terrible, retching movements, her body jack-knifing, her face bare until at last she covered it: 'Those bastards, those bloody bastards.'

Sophy Meister, fortunately, was asleep, her hat off now, her eyes almost as weary with fatigue as the wild woman's. Patience saw that Laura was ashen-faced, she looked as if she might be sick.

'I think I'll get some air,' Laura said. They stood in the corridor among the humped kit-bags of soldiers. They let down the window a crack. The dark fields went by and then a town. Laura thought how complicated it was: they were running away from the Germans, and yet, if that poor woman had known who they were, she would have spat on them. She hoped it wasn't Heini who had bombed that place last night, but if it had been, it wouldn't really be his fault, would it? Someone would have told him to do it? (As someone told him to betray Papa?)

It was like a game of hide-and-seek in an open field with the catcher counting and nowhere to hide.

But school must be all right. An English school.

Then why was she afraid?

Somewhere ahead there must have been an air-raid alarm. The train stopped. A guard came along: they should have had the window shut and the blind down. Didn't they know there was a war on? Patience and Laura went back to their seats. The mad woman slept. The child woke in the soldier's arms and began to whine. At the same moment Sophy Meister stirred, looked around her, dazed, then smiled like an absent-minded hostess who had fallen asleep at her own party. First softly, the soldier began to hum to the child, then to sing, something sweet, something mildly obscene, a barrack-room variation on a popular theme. And as he sang, the child was pacified, and he sang louder, others joined from other carriages like prisoners in their separate cells, until everyone – even the madwoman – was stirred and smiled and joined; until, on a line between stations, in frozen fields, the whole darkened train began to sing.

6

Patience was bored that Laura would keep talking French with Mam'selle. They went into huddles and talked terribly fast and waved their hands around.

'She's even been to tea with her,' Barbara Baxter said.

'She hasn't.'

'I saw them. And Trotty's got a pash on her too, you can tell. She's always calling her back after class and she never gives her detention.' They were in the changing room for hockey. Barbara picked up her stick and hung her captain's whistle round her neck. 'If you ask me, she's fifth column. You know, like a stool-pigeon. Or how did they know Nina had been to the Palais? No one else would have told.'

They walked under the chestnuts towards the muddy pitch. Patience was definitely out of sorts with the world.

'You could have told Miss Mallard.'

'Don't be a fool, Mackenzie. And if you're going to stay in the team, you'd better wake up in goal.'

I hate hockey, thought Patience. I hate being stuck in goal because I'm big. I don't mind being called Patti, or Mac even, sometimes, but I know Barbara only calls people by their surnames because Miss Mallard does. Barbara likes to be called Bobby and that's even sillier. No one else would have told about poor Nina cutting games to go to the tea-dance at the Palais. I wish my father would write, I wish he isn't dead, I wish I was a child and he was there.

Why didn't Laura tell me she'd gone to tea with Mam'selle?

And then there's the play. Laura's sure to get a part, and I'll never see her.

'Shoot!' cried Miss Mallard and the ball crashed against the net. The whistle blew.

. . .

'It is a play,' whispered Miss V. J. Lowrie, 'of longing and disappointment. Chekhov was a great writer and the fact that he was Russian cannot be held against him, since he wrote before the Revolution, and could not have known what rag-tag-and-bobtail were to betray the aspirations of a people aching to be free.' In winter, Miss Lowrie's scarves were woollen, of the finest knit, and she was always wrapping and unwrapping and rewrapping and draping them around her with an air to be envied. Thus she mesmerised the class with hardly any discipline at all. 'You have read *Three Sisters*. I shall be glad of your comments and questions. Rose?'

'I think it's a beautiful play, Miss Lowrie.' Rose blushed, as she did whenever she spoke of or addressed her heroine – she even blushed in her sleep and woke certain that a world with Miss Lowrie in it must surely be a lovely place, after all.

'Thank you, Rose. Barbara?'

'Well, I don't see why, if they wanted to go to Moscow so much, why they didn't just go?'

'Because then, my dear Barbara, this would have been not a tragedy, but a railway timetable. Also, it is a story of the unattainable. We all have our Moscows, our impossible loves, our dreams.' Miss Lowrie, who often took a stroll round the classroom as she taught, brushed the radiators with the tips of her fingers. 'And we must continue to hope: that, I believe, is the message of the ending – that out of our sufferings may come happiness, if not our own, then that of others.' Miss Lowrie carried the book in her hand but had no need to refer to it: ' ". . . our sufferings may mean happiness for the people who come after us . . . There'll be a time when peace and happiness reign in the world, and then we shall be remembered kindly and blessed." A message, indeed, for our times!' As Miss Lowrie spoke it seemed to Rose that the teacher's face was transfigured into one of those lovely portraits of the Madonna they had to colour at the Sacred Heart primary school. Was it sacrilege to think like that, she wondered? Or blasphemy or something? Sometimes she missed the Sacred Heart terribly, but it was true she didn't learn much there and not one of the sisters was a patch on Miss Lowrie.

Nina's hand was up.

'Is it true, Miss Lowrie, we're going to do this with the boys?'

'It is true that this will be a joint production with the Boys' High

School. Miss Winterton has given her permission, provided all meetings and rehearsals take place in our own assembly hall. And that everyone behaves properly, of course. I gave my pledge that you were to be trusted. Patience, please collect the books. The cast list will be pinned on the board on Monday.'

'Why can't we go *there*?' Nina complained, yawning at a contour map of Western Australia. 'I mean, to the Boys' High? Oh Lord, I can never remember if sheep like short grass or is that cows? Does old Winterboots think they're going to rape us?'

They were doing their prep in the conservatory in a lemony winter sun. From here they could see across the playground into the Arboretum, where the camp rose, a tender violet, against the sky.

'Well, we couldn't, could we,' said Rose dreamily, 'we'd have to use their loos?'

'I think the whole thing's stupid,' said Barbara. 'Anyhow, the sixth will get most of the parts.'

Patience sighed. Geography bored her. That is, she loved atlases, with their blue sea, brown mountains and green lowlands, but she could never remember about imports and exports; in Scripture, in the junior school. she had once made a beautiful model of an Old Testament oasis, with the white building and inner courtyard, and palm trees, sand, a little bit of mirror for the water and camels made from twisted pipe-cleaners covered in raffia. That was when she was told she was good with her hands. Her father was in the desert now and she hoped he would find an oasis, but she feared he might not. It seemed to be all sand, that war, with people trying to capture places that did not actually exist, just another part of an endless desert, a dream war of mined, imaginary roads, invented drifting battlefields and poisoned wells.

Rose was saying: 'I know what her initial is. Well, one of them.'

'Whose?'

'V. J. Lowrie.'

'Go on,' groaned Barbara, 'you're going to tell us anyway.'

'D'you really want to know?'

Nina rolled her eyes. 'Passionately!'

'Well. It's V for Violetta in *La Traviata*. You know, the opera.

63

It's the story of the lady of the camellias and it's terribly sad. Miss Lowrie said she might take some of us when the Carl Rosie come.'

'Rosa,' said Patience sharply. 'Not Rosie – Rosa. I saw it last time. It's lovely music but the story's silly. Operas usually are.' Patience didn't mean this, or not altogether: *Traviata* and *La Bohème* both made her blow her nose before the lights went up, because she wanted to cry. Nowadays, for that reason, she always went to opera alone, though she had thought she might ask Laura to come this time. But if Miss Lowrie and a crowd were going to be there, that would spoil everything. She felt downcast. She never talked to anyone about her passion for theatre and opera, because she knew they'd laugh, or not believe her – she simply didn't look that sort of person. She looked like someone who was good at geography. She hadn't spoken the truth now, precisely, for she couldn't be sure if the story didn't move her almost as much as the music; and in any case, she could not separate them. That wonderful awful moment when the father comes on (always from stage right), and then she renounces her lover and you want to shout, No! Don't give in! 'Anyhow,' Patience concluded, 'Violetta dies.'

Rose looked stricken. Patience felt she had been mean and wondered what was the matter with her. Perhaps she was getting the curse. Perhaps she was simply a nasty person.

When the others had gone to break, Nina had to stay in the conservatory-study doing penance for her wild fling at the Palais. Patience too, stayed behind.

'Barbara says that Laura's a Quisling. That she told them about the Palais.'

'Oh, Patti love, you don't believe that!'

'No, of course I don't. No, I don't – really.'

Nina gave her a measuring look. 'Have you two quarrelled or something? You and Laura? Is that what you're so growly about?'

'No, we haven't quarrelled. Honestly, Nina, everything's all right.' Patience changed the subject. 'I wonder who did tell? It's rotten for you.'

'No one, probably,' said Nina. 'I bet Trotty just *knew*. Haven't you noticed – she knows everything. If she were working for the Germans they'd win the war by Christmas.'

'Anyhow, what did happen at the Palais?'

Nina grinned like a cat and flung back her long, dark hair. 'I was raped by a sailor in the foxtrot.'

'The Nina Cherry case,' pondered Claire Winterton. 'You don't think we should have asked for her to be removed?'

Lucy Trott was quite sure. 'Oh no. Harsh punishments for minor crimes debase the currency of discipline. If you hang a man for stealing a sheep, what deterrent remains against murder?' Lucy closed Nina's file. She enjoyed these little meetings all the more in winter, when Claire's heavy grey curtains were drawn and by the light of the green-shaded desk lamp, the two together made the real decisions that affected the life of the school. They would be discussed later in cabinet, in staff-meeting, but really, it was all settled here. 'But it's the end, of course, of her prospects for a prefectship in the sixth.'

Nina's destiny disposed of, there was the matter of Lowrie's cast list for the school play. The Head nodded, then on one name she paused.

'Laura Meister as Irena?'

'I see no harm. If the play is to be done at all. The other major parts come from the sixth, of course, but someone younger seems natural for Irena. And there is something about the Meister girl – she should do quite well.'

The Head nodded and initialled the list, not entirely happily, Lucy could see. It seemed strategic to change the subject.

'There is a sharp decrease in those applying to learn German,' said Lucy.

'An ugly language.'

'I suggest we offer the alternative of Greek.'

They were agreed. But pouring the last, alas, of the even middling sherry, Claire Winterton paused, with the glass in one hand and the decanter in the other.

'My father,' she began. And then she said: 'My father told me once that he could see shadows behind some people, and others had angels on their heads. I can see a shadow behind the Meister girl.'

When Lucy had drunk her sherry, collected her files and left, Claire Winterton was alone in her study. She heard the bell for the end of the day and heard the clatter of feet and the callings of girls in the hall, leaving. Claire went to the window and twitched the long curtains slightly, to make sure that they were closed.

The Head would no more have dreamed of entering the staffroom uninvited than the King of crashing into the Commons, and when she did, Miss Trott, like Black Rod, went before her.

Equally, the staffroom had its own unwritten rules, its hierarchy. Over coffee, Miss Trott took the comfortable seat by the small fire. Miss Lowrie preferred the window-seat with its view of the treetops of the Arboretum and the small heat of the radiator: here she could sit with her knees drawn up and a book on her lap, dreaming of worlds quite other than this shabby room of dun and grey and peeling paint; she had, on the other hand, been a schoolgirl here herself, and never quite got over the privilege of being allowed to walk in without knocking. To walk in at all, indeed, for girls summoned there were interviewed always just outside the door. So, as a girl, she had dreamed of this room as a peasant looks up at Parnassus, and now – what did she dream? Of faery lands forlorn from this casement, and peacocks and silk? She marked homework crisply, in a hand as neat as petit point and dreamed of downy beds, a lover whose face she could not see; and thought in quite a practical way of husbands returning gallantly from war, one of whom she would allow to woo her sweetly. (She wrote letters to some but took care not to commit.) But the watchtower was always there and today it looked especially grim. Very hard in this winter to hold onto sweetness. The play? That might redeem. She had hopes of the German girl. V. J. Lowrie sighed and signed off the last of the exercise books: *a moving essay, of feeling, but please remember that punctuation is one of many rungs on the ladder towards the sublime.*

Josephine Mallard hardly ever sat down. She knocked back her coffee like a pint of beer and paced, smoking furiously. Mam'selle shuddered every time she passed, tried to remember café filtre and forget this cold, hard England: the little Meister girl was a comfort but she worried for her, because she, too, was different and for her it might be worse. I myself, she considered, am *dépaysée*, exiled, but Laura is the true alien, for she has no country at all.

The common room did not always accept the edicts of Winterboot's study.

Jo Mallard challenged Lucy Trott: 'What about this German rubbish?'

'We are offering Greek as an alternative.'

'I think the rest of the senior staff might have been consulted.'

'Very well then, Miss Mallard, I now consult you.'

'And I say that you have not gone far enough. That filthy language should be banned.'

'I wonder,' murmured Lucy Trott, as though proposing an abstract hypothesis, 'if such a ban would be entirely practical in these times?'

'That is not the point. The point is, we should have been consulted.'

'We are back where we started. Tell me, Miss Mallard, were you planning to teach either German or Greek?' The bell rang. Lucy made her exit, threw her last dart from the door: 'I suggest, Miss Mallard, unless you feel yourself capable of running this school, you might stick to hockey. And if those absurd tin soldiers come strutting across the Channel, be grateful that someone is left to speak for us.'

Josephine Mallard was for once struck dumb. She knew herself to be not remarkably intelligent but at least an administrator – yes, surely, that she could do. The school to her had been as certain as a house well built. Now, dimly, she felt it to be undermined, as though the foundations might crumble and the walls secretly fall in, leaving them empty-handed, their mouths blocked by dust. She marched out on to the hockey pitch, blew her whistle and called: 'Upper Third! Take your colours and form up. Two teams! Now!'

They weren't talking about German at all, thought Violetta Lowrie, they were talking about the Meister girl.

By the time Miss Lowrie too had followed the bell to her next class, Mam'selle had looked all around her like a nervous mouse in a cat-basket, settled her small, arthritic bones into Lucy Trott's fireside chair and fallen asleep, her wig, tipped over her nose, rising and falling as her breath came out in little puffs.

There were warnings now any time of night or day, but less damage than in some provincial cities. Derby bore the brunt. A couple of times a day though, the girls might find themselves herded by Miss Mallard to the shelter. Walk fast, she would cry, don't run. Click, clack, thought Patience, Death's trim men, but somehow, as they marched across the autumn grass – some goose-stepping to annoy – she felt none of this to be entirely real. This was not war: war was that long journey with the Meisters; war was both clear and distant – like a train seen across fields, going into the dark.

In the shelter, it was quite fun, if you got someone decent like Miss Lowrie or Mam'selle, who let you talk instead of working. The lights were so dim it was difficult to work anyway. There were four shelters, each named by a colour so that you knew which one to go to. Miss Mallard, the Himmler of the shelters, had worked out as many rules as possible to make life uncomfortable, but there were all kinds of ways of getting round them. You could smuggle in a *Girls' Crystal*, for instance, under your jumper or inside an exercise book; and while everyone was supposed to have a colour and always go to the same shelter, they found quite soon that as long as you were inside, and avoided Mallard's own shelter, and you had your gas-mask, no one seemed to care what colour you were. Because of being a prefect – even though only second-grade, fifth-form – Patience didn't like to, but she knew Nina and some of the others occasionally avoided the shelters altogether. When they went to the cloakroom to get their gas-masks and coats, they simply ducked into the boiler-room and stayed there. In fact, they were probably safer there than in the shelter – provided Mallard didn't do one of her surprise round-ups and Barbara Baxter didn't tell.

One awful thing happened in the shelter. Someone started to scream and went on screaming and it was when Mallard was there. It was Posy Potter who had claustrophobia. Rose put her arm round her but she went on screaming until Mallard shook her and slapped her face. Then she collapsed on Rose, weeping.

Mallard announced: 'No one is to leave this shelter until the all-clear. *No one*, under any circumstances. Is that understood?'

Patience looked away. She felt ashamed of something, though of what she could not have said.

She was ashamed because Mallard was right? Because Posy could have set off some sort of hysteria beneath these walls and roof of earth and iron? Laura beside her, looked pale. Patience had hardly seen her properly for days, and wondered if she was getting an asthma attack.

'Are you all right?'

'Yes.' Laura nodded. 'Just a bit of Posy's trouble. It's better if I take deep breaths.' She breathed and smiled. 'I haven't seen you for ages. I thought you were angry with me.'

They had to whisper, and pretend to read.

'I'm sorry. I'm really sorry. I was being stupid. I'm terribly glad you've got that part in the play. Is your father all right? He's so nice. Has he got to stay at that place?'

'Well, he might be moved. It might be better. I'm not sure. It's something to do with his work. We don't really know.'

'You'll be very good as Irena.'

'Oh, I'd love that if I could do it!' Then Laura's faced closed again, as it sometimes did, as though she had shut a door and locked it behind her and entered a dark and secret room.

All clear.

They walked out of the shelter into brilliant darkness: full moon, bombers' moon, frost shining on every twig and branch.

Laura said: 'I don't think they like us being friends, very much.'

Those rehearsing for the play were excused the Friday afternoon games period from three till four, once a week. Mallard, of course, was outraged by this, but what could she do about it? After-school activities were out of the question, as things stood in the world. Not easily beaten, she campaigned for compulsory dinner-time netball for the actresses. Failed again.

Miss Mallard often felt that if she were given command, she would run the war quite differently. She was lonely, she feared idle hands. Men had all the fun in war. She felt the same about the school: that if Lucy Trott were not always in the way, she could persuade the Head to tighten up. She'd got halfway there with the Meister girl until Trott intervened. The Head was weak, she was clay in the wrong hands. Miss Mallard had a bed-sitting-room on Derby Road with gas ring and share of bathroom. Her family was in Surrey and her brothers were in the war. She volunteered for fire-watching at Albert Lodge. She could keep an eye on things. An ear, too, for after a week of sleeping on a camp-bed in the boiler-room (between intermittent torchlight patrols), she became convinced that all was not as it should be: there was a night prowler in Albert Lodge! A torch suddenly extinguished, a rustle from an empty room. Smoking furiously and drinking cocoa from her flask in the boiler-room, Mallard decided to bide her time: here, at last, she had something to take to the Head, and the Head would have to listen.

Patience had noticed before that as rehearsals got under way there was a crackle of tension in the school that broke out sometimes into hysteria. As scenery painter and general provider of props – her apparently preordained role – she saw it from both sides. The anxiety among the cast within, and outside, especially among the younger ones, an increase in pashes and a lot of stupid hanging around as though the actors had somehow put on golden robes and become kings and queens. Almost, Patience understood, since in the real theatre she had felt that herself and still did; once, she'd got Donald Wolfit's autograph and slept with it under her pillow. She was older now, haunted stage-doors no more, but the wonder remained, that people in other respects perfectly ordinary, stepped onstage and assumed a powerful mystery.

And, where there was mystery and passion, there was violence.

Long before the one and only performance, scheduled for a January afternoon (Hitler permitting), factions formed and fought with the bloody single-mindedness of pubescent girls and warlike nations. Laura – as Patience had predicted – collected a trail of followers. Who were found one day cracking heads with Barbara's team of hockey fiends. Both armies were patched up, ticked off and deprived of privileges, which served, of course, only to stiffen their enmity and their passion.

·   ·   ·

70

Laura seemed not to notice any of this. She was worried about her mother she said, who could not get some medicine or other. And when the boys arrived for the first joint play-reading, in early December, Laura was putting on her waifs-and-strays face, her drowned sparrow act.

One day, Patience and Miss Trott arrived at the same moment in the empty form room.

There, scrawled in chalk on the board, was the message: LAURA MEISTER IS A JEW.

Patience gasped. Miss Trott's face was expressionless. She sat at her desk and set out her papers.

'Clean the board, please, Patience.'

The board wiped, Patience settled behind her desk in the front row. She could still feel the chalk on her hands. Her face, she knew, was burning. She opened a book and pretended to read. She wanted desperately to wash her hands, and then she wanted to find whoever had done this and hurt them. Her hands shook. She blurted out: 'But it's not even true! They were running away from Hitler, but not because they're Jews!'

Miss Trott sighed and seemed to take a decision. She was already wearing her winter mittens but sinus had now replaced hay fever as her torment and no amount of inhalers seemed to do the trick. How she longed for the sun, sun without pollen, without Claire's flowers, a chalkless place beneath the sun, a place, in particular, that did not contain young girls. Sometimes she felt that, when she was tired. But she liked Patience Mackenzie.

'Will you come to my house this afternoon, for a little while, if your mother will not be worried?'

The Edwardian villa across the road was like a burrow and Miss Trott inhabited it as some small, waterside animal might hole up for the winter. A modest fire was stoked and puffed to life. The chairs were small, so were the cups and plates. Patience thought of Mrs Tiggywinkle but the resemblance to her form teacher went no further than the furnishings. The scene was cosy. The circumstances were not.

'I take it, Patience, that you have spoken to no one about this morning's disgusting graffiti?' Patience shook her head. She had avoided Laura all day and just stopped herself telling Nina.

'Then in that case it can be forgotten.'

'But it's so awful. How can we forget it?'

'Because there is nothing we can do about it. And we know it to be untrue.'

'But if it were true?' Patience remembered uneasily the Odessa grocers.

'Then there would still be nothing we could do. History, you will find, is an inexorable process. We can neither halt nor alter it. No one knows that so well as our friends, the Jews.' Miss Trott looked into the teapot and found it empty. 'And there is something else, Patience. I have been glad to see you help Laura, but sometimes in a small society like ours, we have to guard against sentimental attachments. You understand?'

No! No, I understand nothing at all if I can't be with Laura, see her, help her.

They make it sound filthy.

'I think I should go now, Miss Trott. It's nearly dark.'

'And now, my dear girl, I've upset you.' The teacher plucked the small black kettle from the fire with a kettle-holder, and filled the teapot. 'Please sit down again, Patience.'

Patience felt like a giant in this room of doll's furniture. She felt awkward, destructive, angry. Miss Trott sat back, removed the spectacles that she wore on a string round her neck, and pinched the bridge of her nose, a sign of contemplation. She looked tired, drained dry, as exhausted as Patience had ever seen her.

'Patience, have you ever known me to be unfair?'

'No, Miss Trott.' Oddly, that was true.

'And you know I think highly of Laura Meister, as I do of you. I would not ask you to abandon her. She is in a peculiar position in our little society and needs friends. I'll admit to you because you are a sensible girl, to be trusted, that Miss Winterton had doubts. However. These are difficult times. There is a rash mood around, I sense that now more than ever we must guard against folly. I would like to see you at Oxford, Patience. Nothing must spoil your chances, nothing – silly.' Miss Trott spoke the last word as though picking a bad plum out of a bowl. 'And now you must run home.'

Patience did run. It was foul, it was horrible. She ran and all she could think was Laura, Laura! Nearer home, she slowed her step and took deep breaths. She wanted to bath, to scrub herself all over and then bath again. Even Spring Gardens, that had always been so consoling, so sure, with its clipped hedges and good dogs, was as dark now as the rest of the world.

Miss Lowrie, in her element, wore pigeon-blue with a lace collar and a little cameo brooch at the throat. At three o'clock on a Friday afternoon, the boys trooped into the assembly hall looking clean and embarrassed. They sat in a circle of chairs – a half-moon of girls and the same of boys – and read their parts, eyes down, stumbling sometimes over the Russian names. Cordelia King from the sixth read Olga (she was supposed to be going to RADA and was frightfully rich and was seen in the Kardomah on a Saturday morning wearing a fur coat) but the fifth-formers got more than they had expected – something to do with sixth-form exams. In spite of the terrible episode of the Palais tea-dance, Nina was Masha and was rather good, Patience thought, not a bit actressy and talking as she always did of love and clothes. And Laura, of course, as Irena, the youngest. She looked dowdy today, rather down, but the moment she got to the first big speech something electric, rather creepy happened. '"Really, I don't know why there's such joy in my heart. I remembered this morning that it was my Saint's day, and suddenly I felt so happy, and I thought of the time when we were children, and Mother was still alive. And then such wonderful thoughts came to me, such wonderful stirring thoughts!"' At the end of her speech there was a silence – even Cordelia King couldn't follow that. Laura was not playing Irena, she *was* Irena; and Moscow seemed a thousand miles away and they'd never get there, yet Irena was the only one who would never accept that. Never!

Into the silence, Miss Lowrie dropped a scarf.

That first time there were cocoa and buns to break the ice. With Patience's help, Miss Lowrie served like a hostess dispensing champagne and caviar.

'And now!' she said, clapping her hands, 'everyone must get to know everyone. Mingle! Mix!'

The boys looked at Miss Lowrie and fell in love with her. The boys looked at the girls and the girls at the boys. Nina broke the ice with a couple of her swains and quite soon she and Miss Lowrie were comfortably settled in their separate courts. Laura had spoken to Miss Lowrie before the cocoa was handed out, and slipped away. Something to do with her mother, Patience supposed. She poured her own cocoa and found a boy standing beside her.

'Can I help?' He was quite tall, with fair hair, a nice face.

'That's all right. I've finished now. Thanks.'

'Then let's sit down.' He smiled. 'I'm Toozenbach. The rest of my name's unpronounceable.'

'Yes, I know. You're a baron. I'm Patience Mackenzie.'

'D'you come in later?'

'No, I'm the sort of dog's-body, you know. Scenery, that sort of thing. I don't mind. I like it.'

'My real name's Stephen Marlowe.'

'I've seen you before.'

'Oh, Lord, not that ghastly OTC? We feel absolute idiots.'

'No. It was in the summer. When you were playing cricket. The last day of term. I remember because you reminded me of someone's brother. I mean, you might have been him – you're so alike.'

'Well, they say everyone has a *doppelgänger*. You know, we've all got a double walking around somewhere. Bit creepy. Who is this chap?'

'I've never seen him. Just his photograph.'

Stephen nodded. He seemed shy, yet Patience didn't feel he was bored. There was a silence though, and somehow she didn't want him to get up and go away, she wanted to keep him with her. The others were beginning to stack their mugs on a tray. Nina was fooling around and there was a roar of laughter. He would go. Patience wanted to pluck him back.

'Irena was very good? You know, Laura, the one with the dark hair.'

'She was. She was marvellous, made the rest of us look feeble.' He glanced round. 'She's not here now, is she. What happens to her in the end? In the play, I mean? We haven't read right through yet.'

'You fall in love with her.'

It was a crisp, dry evening, a waxing moon. The voices of the girls and boys carried clearly, calling good night. Love, thought Patience, swinging her heavy satchel, amour, amore, an opera word. Love was for theatre, for poor Toozenbach . . . oh, how she loved theatre! There had been a warning and now came the thump of guns from the Castle, searchlights fingering the sky. But they called out cheerfully enough, the youngsters running for shelter: good night; and they did not run very fast because they liked the clean trumpet sound of their voices in the air – good night, good night!

7

There was war in heaven. Those below could hear the clash of swords but security was always tight. Posy Potter, who knew things inaudible to the human ear (presumably on the dog whistle principle) was ordered to tune into the ether. She sat in the boiler-room, with her hands over her eyes, rocking, but nothing came through and they did not like to push her further in case of a fit. In the end it was Barbara Baxter who announced with great importance, one wet dinner-break in the form room: 'Miss Mallard's caught a prowler. At night. And you'll never guess who it is.'

'Poor old Bill the Boiler, I suppose,' said Nina. 'Everyone knows about him. It's mouldy if they're making a fuss about that.'

'No, not Bill.'

Nina yawned. 'Oh well then, go on, tell us. You're going to anyway.'

'Miss Trott! Your precious Trotty lets herself in at night and snoops. Mallard caught her. She went straight to the Head.'

'Don't believe you. Don't see that it matters anyway.'

'She might get the sack. Miss Winterton's very upset.'

'It was for you, my dear Claire,' said Lucy Trott. 'I am your eyes. You know that. And your ears.'

The Head turned away from the tall window behind her desk, from the slanting rain. Such a sorrowful day.

'Lucy, what would I do without you? But perhaps we could be a little more discreet? Shall we pull the curtains? That camp is such a blot on the landscape, it quite spoils the Arboretum. Now tell me, how is the play going? The German girl?'

'Laura Meister is working out very well. As I expected. Quite brilliant I am told. But you might have been right, after all. That's a situation that needs watching.'

'I am sure that I can rely on you for that, Lucy,' the Head replied with unusual crispness.

For the first time she could recall, Lucy Trott felt herself to be dismissed. As she left the study, she had a vague sense of having been threatened, or of having promised something.

Winter. Christmas. Posy's chilblains in full flower, a cold season; with the first snow the Arboretum was transformed to a world of glinting white and in the camp the prisoners kicked a football around in a blizzard. Cautiously, the girls had moved a little closer to the camp, not to stare, but because the camp drew them, and they were sorry for the men. At least, at Christmas they could be sorry.

Nina tried to throw them some chocolate, behind the guard's back, but it missed; the second time she had the brilliant idea of volleying it over the high fence with a tennis racket, and it landed safely. Patience felt uncomfortable: it was too much like feeding animals in a zoo. The prisoners were pleased though, and one of them called out to the girls.

'What did he say?'

'Happy Christmas,' said Laura.

Nina waved. 'That one's rather sweet.' She hopped up and down with cold. 'What's he saying now?'

'He likes your legs.'

The guard noticed but seemed tolerant. Except for Laura, the girls edged closer to the fence. They could see the men's faces now, make out their features, the details of their clothing, the rough worn jackets, a button astray, chilled hands, a few wearing mittens. The girls became suddenly shy at the press of faces on the other side and even Nina backed away. They were too close, they were people, it was awful. Some of the younger men pulled kissing faces; the older ones looked not dangerous, but tired, grey-faced and somehow foolish, like the larger, sadder animals Patience had thought of in a zoo, or grown men in a school playground. The girls felt they had done something they should not have done. They turned and ran. The men watched them go silently, and that was how Patience saw them when she glanced back: a blur once again without identity – prisoners.

After prayers, as she read out school notices the next morning in the assembly hall, Miss Winterton announced in the same tone she might have spoken of a hockey fixture: 'It is understood that no girl of this school will at any time or for any reason consort with or give succour to the enemy. In view of the weather netball is cancelled. Please report to the gymnasium for all games periods.'

'Who *told* her?'
'Someone sneaked.'
'Well, they saw us, silly. From the staffroom.'
'Trotty? It's still sneaking. Or Mallard more likely.'
'It could have been Winterboots from her study.'
'They never told us we couldn't.'
'That's why we're not being punished.'
'I didn't like it, anyway.'
'Mmn.' Nina nodded and stretched. 'I suppose I have got quite nice legs.'

But the play. Right through that season of snow and war and Christmas, those involved lived for the play, it seemed to redeem everything. For Patience, that horrid and mysterious conversation with Miss Trott about Laura, which Laura had, even more mysteriously, foretold. For Laura, to step on to the stage, to forget herself and take on Irena, was to enter an enchanted world far from the twilight room to which she must return, where her mother moaned for her drugs, and sometimes she could get them and sometimes she could not; and there was the sickly invalid smell, the sense of darkness pressing in on them, the terrible absence of her father, the

78

presence of her mother's broken life which implored Laura, and to which she could not respond. This England was not pretty at all, that could house that dark room, and the camp, and her father's camp and the darkness over that city they passed in the train, that had been bombed. Then one day she would get home and find Maman bright, too bright, up and properly dressed, the curtains open, the room haphazardly dusted, every lamp lit, and tea laid out before the fire. Perhaps there would be a letter from Papa, potato cake in the oven, and Maman would kiss her on both cheeks and say: 'We are lucky to be alive!' Then holding her at arm's length: 'But you are drab, my little sparrow, we must find you a bright new red dress, *ma pauvre petite*. That horrible uniform! What the English do to their children!' Then Laura would have to explain again about the blackout, and pull the curtains. She knew quite well they hadn't enough coupons for a dress of any kind (and she was too young for her mother's Paris models). Sometimes, not loving her mother very much, Laura felt herself to be the wickedest person in the world.

On one of her interesting Paris walks with Scotty, they had entered a Popish cathedral at Christmas (sightseeing in hell, as Scotty put it, though part of Laura's family was Catholic anyway); and Laura had overheard a priest in a box with curtains tell a veiled woman: 'We feel guilty for the damage inflicted upon us. We are all conspirators with our sufferings.'

Laura thought about that now, and wondered.

The boys and the girls had got easier together, the more they became absorbed in the play. In the Christmas spirit someone put up a sprig of mistletoe and Jack Cardington, who played a dashing Soliony, kissed Miss Lowrie for a dare. He was a tall, handsome boy with shiny black hair, both joker and putative seducer, and it was clear that Miss Lowrie did not mind at all.

'What about the three sisters?' someone called. So then it was the turn of Nina (who did not resist), then Cordelia King and Laura. Cordelia took it like a queen, as her due, while Laura, grinning wickedly, averted her head at the last moment to take it on the cheek.

'Come on, Marlowe, your turn,' Jack called, but Stephen coloured and smiled, shook his head. Miss Lowrie meanwhile had reasserted authority.

'We must get this last scene right. From Chebutykin's entrance, please.' Miss Lowrie clasped her hands. 'And Olga, could we have, do you suppose, a little more *yearning*?'

Patience retired to the little room behind the stage where props and wardrobe were assembled: her responsibility. She could hear the muffled voices from the stage. Concentrating on the job of transforming someone's grannie's nightie into a pretty dress for Irena, she jumped when Stephen Marlowe spoke.

'You're doing a terribly good job. I don't know how you get all this stuff.'

'Laura brought some. Her mother used to be very smart – well she still is – but some of her things are out of date or she doesn't like them any more. I can make the hems longer you see, and pull in the waist. It's a pity Laura can't have them, but people don't dress like that any more. They're beautiful materials – look, that's a Worth label! It seems awful cutting them up.'

Patience smiled. She did like the fabrics – especially Mrs Meister's tea dress with the spludged roses and trailing sleeves (fancy dressing up for tea!). What a pity she couldn't use them all. The sisters did seem to wear rather dull clothes and Masha wore black all the time. She liked Stephen Marlowe too. He wasn't the same as the others, fooling around, he didn't mind sitting still. He didn't expect you to say clever things.

Tarara-boom-di-ay . . . I'm sitting on a tomb-di-ay

Poor old Chebutykin, his falling hair, he had been in love with their mother and no one ever took any notice of him. Patience thought he was the nicest person in the play.

'Oh dear, Miss Lowrie's stopped him again.'

'Well, he does sound as if he's doing "Knees up Mother Brown".'

Patience went on sewing.

'D'you think he's supposed to be cheerful or sad at the end? Chebutykin?'

'What do you think?'

Patience laid down her sewing for a moment. 'I think he's someone who once wanted something very much, but he didn't get it, and he hasn't wanted anything since. So he just hums to himself, doesn't care. There are lots of people like that.'

'But if they're rehearsing, shouldn't you be up there?'

'Last act. I'm dead.'

And then, at the last rehearsal before Christmas, the first run through, with lights though not yet costumes, Jack Cardington brought cider and everything became rather fun. Barbara Baxter – in spite of her contempt for the whole business – smoothly lowered the curtain, raised it again for the curtain call, then dropped it for the last time.

Patience and Miss Lowrie, and the few others seeing it right through for the first time, clapped; the curtain fell; more clapping – the curtain rose for the cast to take their bows, then fell. Patience thought, with the clothes, with the props, it will be magic.

Beside her, Violetta Lowrie sighed triumphantly: 'I do believe it will be all right. It could be lovely!'

A few times in the Christmas holidays some of the cast met up, mostly at the Kardomah, once at the Palais. Usually, it would be Jack Cardington who got them together and they were generally Nina, Jack, Patience, Stephen and Laura. It was fun. They were for that short season, a gang, a group; they were, at fifteen or sixteen or so, free for the first time to squeal with laughter as they danced down the street, to run around town. Jack made them all do the palais glide on the frozen lake in the Arboretum, in the dance-hall one afternoon he performed with Laura a most remarkable tango. The spotlight was on them, the rest fell back.

'Where did Laura learn to do that?' Stephen marvelled.

'In Paris. Her governess taught her.'

Laura came back to the table, gasping for breath, but shining, excited: 'Come on, Stephen, your turn!'

'Sorry, I can't.' He smiled and coloured. It became another of their games: making Stephen blush.

Patience thought that was unfair: he was rather sweet. Serious too, like Heini in the picture. Their way home was the same – to Spring Gardens – and one night he told Patience how he wanted to be a scientist, was good at physics, middling at chemistry and worried about his maths.

'Why do you want to? Be a scientist, I mean.'

'It sounds silly. I want to be an astronomer.'

'That's not silly.'

They walked on. The stars crackled in the cold sky. They sat for a moment on a low wall and Stephen mapped the heavens for her: the Plough, the Bear, Orion's belt, Betelgeuse, Venus. Patience was enchanted, as though someone had opened a door for her and shown her a whole new world. She could not hear enough, but the siren went and they had to run home. She was dizzy with stars. She wished Laura had been there.

Christmas snow. White Christmas. Mary Mackenzie and Patience shared a small black-market chicken, and later would boil up the bones. In the afternoon, Patience did not like to leave her mother, so they listened to the King, then played Monopoly. There was no raid that day. Everything was very still and quiet, white. There was no movement across the land outside the city; within, a little traffic, a few brave pedestrians come out to view this new-made world – the snowfall bestowed grace, muffled pain. In the Cathedral boys in white and red followed the Cross up the aisle and, frozen, sang like angels, their clear voices, fearful of breaking, telling the half a dozen gathered and listeners at the door, that the child was born in the manger and there was no death; not in the earth nor the sky, nor the privy dark room nor narrow bed. Death too shall die!

They are lying, thought Laura, following her mother out of the Cathedral. They always do lie.

Lucy Trott and Claire Winterton shared a small cut of beef. Claire cooked and carved. Claire was getting rather bossy. She talked about Christmas in the rectory and gave Lucy the gristle.

The camp was no longer a charcoal scrawl. As the snow settled on every post and fence and hut – anything hard or dark or sharp – and falling, froze, the camp became just another part of a wide, white, frozen landscape.

There were rumours that one city was being disguised as another, and they were to get Derby's bombs, but it was only a rumour and though air-raid warnings continued day and night, nothing too dreadful happened. Patience thought this was a peculiar sort of war – their part of it, at least. Thousands of miles away, battles being fought, terrible events, her father, Laura's brother, Nina's two brothers; yet from here often all they saw was a glow in the sky as though someone had lit bonfires all around them. There were the distant guns, muffled, and closer, from the castle, the sound like someone slamming the door behind him. Though they were forced to live as if in permanent danger of extinction, the real war appeared most of the time to be taking place just off-stage. When there was a daytime dog-fight in the sky, everyone in Spring Gardens came out on their lawns to watch and called their children. The next day the younger ones went hunting for shrapnel. They found nothing. The snow covered it.

And with the snow, even that aspect of the war – the overflying bombers – ceased for the moment and the city was wrapped in a white, feathery peace. The play could go on and on it went quite wonderfully, beyond expectations, fulfilling all Miss Lowrie's brightest hopes and contradicting, flatly, all doubters.

Perhaps it was well done. Perhaps it was the right time, the right weather, the right mood for this play, but from the first moment, even before the curtain rose, when every prop was miraculously in place and Patience could hear the audience, like an animal waiting, its breath warm, and went back to check the girls' costumes (the boys had to do the best they could in the gym), she knew that there would be magic. There was the Prozorovs' ballroom, with luncheon laid and sunshine outside (Barbara was good on lights as well as curtains), and in the passageway between the gym and the hall she found Laura, wandering in her transformed nightdress. They whispered, as though they might be heard from the hall.

'Hurry up. You're on!'

'Yes, of course. I was just a bit scared.'

'No need to be.'

Irena had them. It was like love; or infatuation, rather: the sudden attention from the dutiful and cold-footed audience, the moment she came on. She threw them an enchanted thread, she played them. Alone, centre stage, *Moscow! Moscow! Moscow!* Then poor Toozenbach dead because she couldn't love him or because she might have done, at last the three sisters together and at the very last that jaunty band coming in only half a minute late. Even Her Highness Cordelia King seemed to sense and respond to the sweet, desolate power Laura brought every time she stepped onstage: '"There'll be a time when peace and happiness reign in the world . . ."' And that *tarara*: quiet, no more than a hum, a lullaby – right at the last, *tarara*, old Chebutykin singing himself to sleep.

The audience was transported, silenced, then the applause began and went on and on, through one curtain, then two, then three. And then the cry, 'Irena!' and Laura stepped out of the line for one quick bow alone. Patience had slipped into the front row to watch. From here she could see their painted faces and more than one safety-pin and yet her friends on the stage were still those strange and wonderful creatures: actors, gods come to earth.

In the classroom that served as a dressing-room and that smelled so deliciously of greasepaint, even Miss Winterton looked down briefly from her frozen peak to say that everyone had done well, really very well. Mam'selle was in tears, her wig as askew as her English at this moving moment, seizing and drenching Laura in French praise. Lucy Trott widened her eyes at this Gallic excess, and, ordering the stage, gym, classroom and props room to be cleared by seven, followed in Miss Winterton's wake. No one was upset. That was simply Trotty, that was her way.

And Violetta Lowrie – while not a drencher like Mam'selle, mopped a damp eye with a trailing, scented handkerchief and could not speak, it was too much. An ever-longing dreamer for other lands, she had found, for once, perfection on her own doorstep. Lucy Trott, for whom she had respect, had warned her long ago: avoid favour. Always remember they go, we stay. Was this favour? To be so moved? Next year, other little girls, yet surely never again anything to match this unlooked-for joy. Smiling, she spread her arms.

In front of the mirror, Laura scrubbed off her make-up hurriedly. Her eyes looked bruised, hollow and brilliant. On the desk before her a bunch of flowers in florist's paper needed water.

Patience said: 'I couldn't see your mother?'

'She's not there.'

'There's cocoa for everyone.'

'Can't stop.'

'You were frightfully good.'

Their eyes met in the mirror, then Laura's gaze flickered away. She pulled on that awful old drab coat with the ratty collar and got up to go.

'Something's happened,' said Laura in a low voice. 'You see, we got a letter through Switzerland today, it may have taken months. Heini's been shot down. He might not be dead but he's missing. And now I must hurry. I shouldn't have left Maman.'

'Oh, Laura! Can I come? Can I help?'

'Not tonight. Bless you Patti.' Laura's lips brushed Patience's cheek, and then she was gone.

Patience felt sorry for the flowers, even if they were dingy old chrysanths. She stuck them, paper and all, in a jug of drinking water no one would need any more. She stayed to help clear up the stage. How shabby it all looked now, in the ordinary light. The verandah was going and the garden chairs and the paper plants. Patience touched her cheek. She walked for the last time in the Prozorovs' garden.

Tara.

Part Two

8

June.

Lucy Trott stood at the Head's window, looking down on to the playground. With the abrupt change of direction favoured by a threatened queen on a chessboard, she had adjusted her opinion.

'There are some rather hysterical factions forming. Netball seems to have become Barbara Baxter's cohorts versus the aesthetes. Blood was drawn at hockey, I believe. And Mallard is insisting that Laura Meister must play. Her asthma seems improved. Mallard's side has the muscle, of course. I begin to think you were right, Claire. It was not a good day for the school when we took her on.'

'The German girl? Oh, I don't think it has been disastrous yet – she did make a pretty Irena. If there is any danger, it could be to her.'

'What form would you expect it to take?'

'Oh, you know quite well what I mean, Lucy. Any society has its natural victims. And if the German girl is having her little triumph now, remember your myths: the victim is frequently elevated before slaughter.'

'It will not come to *that*,' said Miss Trott, with some of her old sharpness. There were times when she wondered if Claire quite had her feet on the ground, if she were not too head-in-the-clouds to have charge of two hundred lively, growing girls. More than once she had subdued the heretical fantasy that Claire might be a little dotty. No harm there, of course, if she stayed in the clouds, but lately she had begun to meddle, to have opinions. Lucy, who had always been her *praefectus*, wondered if Claire might be getting intelligence from another source?

'I'm sorry, Head, what did you say?'

'I said, he appears not to be arriving after all. A tactical error.'

'Who?'

'Herr Hitler. The Russian front is a mistake. Ask Napoleon.'

So summer gathered. Not a scorcher like last year, but there was a smell of green in the air and the sky was wonderfully empty of all but barrage balloons. Even now, five months after, Laura was still a star, little girls were in love with her though she hardly noticed; and someone chalked on her locker: *Juden raus*. Also, inside her desk lid, a swastika.

'Well, she can't be *both*,' said Nina, 'that's ridiculous. I mean, her father had to run away from Hitler, didn't he?'

Patience nodded. The truth about Heini, even his existence, had been kept from everyone. Perhaps Trotty knew, but she knew everything.

Patience could see how painful these months had been for her friend; to mourn and keep her mourning secret, even from her father who would still not hear his son's name spoken; and all this time not to know if Heini were alive or dead. Mrs Meister had been quiet – too quiet – and that was another worry for Laura.

As for the graffiti, Laura had said something rather peculiar. When she first saw them, she looked ill, but now she had recovered and they were sitting on the terrace wall, gazing out over the thickening green towards the camp. A subtly different place from last year: now the prisoners had planted lettuce, ferny-headed carrots and even flowers – bright, orange-faced marigolds. Blankets flapped on a clothes-line and every morning the prisoners did physical jerks. One of them, gardening, stripped off his shirt. On such a day it was noticeable how ordinary the place had become. Another day, in rain or under a grey sky, it looked what it was, a cage, alarming, reminding; but at this moment it almost seemed as though these were simply people, getting on with their own lives in a corner of war, as does happen. All these men lacked was the right to walk out.

Laura let her book rest in her lap. 'Sometimes I wish I were. A Jew. A proper one, then I'd know who I was. About one quarter of a fingernail of me is Jewish and even that much worries Maman. And, of course, I wouldn't really want it. We've lost so many of our friends – especially Papa's friends from the university – and then when they

90

came for him here, in the night, in England, I thought it must be like that for the Jews.

'But still, it would make you feel real, as though you had a country you carried in your head. Scotty thought a lot of the Jews. When Maman wasn't around she used to tell me all about the diaspora – when they were all scattered two thousand years ago – and how they hope to go home to Palestine, and all about the Balfour declaration. Sometimes she took me to see a weird old man in the *Marché des Puces*: he had black robes and long greasy ringlets. He sold ancient books and they used to talk for hours in French and a bit of Russian Scotty had picked up. He frightened me at first, but then I got used to him. Scotty said he was a scholar. He took us to the shop behind his stall once, and gave us tea in glasses. I asked Scotty, if he was a scholar, like my father, what was he doing working in the flea-market, and she said I was an ignorant child and to hush my tongue.'

'What happened to him?'

'I don't know,' said Laura. 'He stayed behind, like Scotty.'

The bell went and they walked slowly back to the classroom.

Patience said: 'English Jews seem rather boring.'

'Phrases to be learned by heart,' said Miss Trott, sneezing at a butterfly: '*Me fortem praebeo. Evita excedo.* Patience?'

'I show myself brave. I depart from this life.'

'Rose!' Rose jumped. She had caught a stolen glimpse of Miss Lowrie in forget-me-not blue crossing the playground. 'I'm sorry, Miss Trott, what did you say?'

'*We are free daughters of Britain.* Transcribe by tomorrow. Also *Pain is felt by all mortals.* And Caesar, pages twenty to twenty-one.' She swept from the room, leaving behind a faint scent of camphor.

Rose groaned. 'I thought we'd finished with soppy *Juliana*. Though Caesar's worse, of course. What do his stupid old wars matter anyway? He was just like Hitler, a greedy pig.'

'I think,' Barbara announced, 'Trott's losing her grip. She's out of favour with Winterboots.'

'Oh, shut up,' said Nina. 'Your Mallard's a duck anyway. Quack! Quack!'

Barbara Baxter coloured. 'You wait, Nina Cherry.'

'And what?'

That summer day, in the boiler-room, one small and bewildered follower of the aesthetes – that is, a third-former who worshipped the triumvirate of Laura, Patience and Nina – was given a bloody nose. She told matron she had run into a door.

All this, while her heroines disported themselves with Jack Cardington and Stephen Marlowe in the Arboretum maquis. Barbara no longer came, but ever since the play these three, and sometimes Rose, had taken to meeting the boys most fine days. Sometimes they had a picnic, sometimes they talked. There was very little real flirtation, even from Jack; just the girls and boys in the greening and secret shrubbery. In a dreary lesson, on a rainy day, even when she had long left this place behind, Patience's mind could conjure that circular clearing, the golden finger of sunlight through the trees, a flash of illicit bluebells and the tight-fisted rhododendron buds slowly opening into blazing, improbable beauty; too waxy, too rich somehow, they seemed to have strayed from the tropics – hothouse blooms in a prim English shade.

The ground was peaty and warm. Long Jack, the sybarite, lay with his legs stretched out and demanded an apple, peeled and sliced. If Rose was around, he usually got one and, eyes closed, accepted it: 'Oh, Rosie Posie, pudding and pie, bless you for mercy to a starving soul! Give us a kiss?'

'I won't then.'

Jack propped himself on one elbow. 'I say, are you girls going to that farming camp thing?' His hand encircled Nina's ankle.

Nina kicked and grinned. 'Probably, end of July. Are you?'

'We're more or less conscripted. Not so bad if you're going though. Lust among the sukebind?'

Stephen said: 'You do talk a lot of rot, Cardy. It'll be like monks and nuns, anyway.'

'You ought to know, old chum.'

'Oh, shut up, Cardy.'

Stephen was still shy, easily teased, and seemed most comfortable with Patience. She remembered when he had told her about the stars and liked it when he talked to her, the sound of his voice, his hesitations, his excitement on the rare occasions he mentioned his work.

One day, when the others were fooling around, Stephen asked Patience: 'This chap you know who looked like me. Were you in love with him?'

'Heavens, no. I don't even know him. And I've never been in love. Have you?'

'I'm not sure. I don't think so. You're very nice, Patience.'

Nice, she thought. *Nice*! What a thing to be.

Once, she saw Jack and Laura laughing about something and Stephen watching them.

Another time, Jack came in triumph with a bottle of cider, on a very hot day. Stephen drank a little more than the others and fell asleep. Rose and Nina collected bluebells and bracken and arranged them upon his head and in his hair and on his chest. He looked so unguarded sleeping there.

'I think he looks absolutely bee-ootiful,' said Rose, sighing and dreaming of lovely funerals.

Laura too had slept. She woke and saw what they had done.

'Take them off,' she said sharply. 'It looks like a bier. It looks as if he were dead.'

Whatever the game was, it was finished for that day. There was no more fun, that time.

Since the news about Heini, it was different now at the Meisters'. At first Patience had felt she shouldn't go, she would be an intruder, even though Laura asked her, said she would cheer up her mother. Oddly, it was her own mother – who spoke usually of things, hardly ever of feelings – who remarked, while she sewed by the fire and Patience did her homework at her father's desk:

'You haven't been to the Meisters' lately?'

'I don't think I ought to butt in.'

Her mother's look was measuring. Then she turned to her sewing again, and pulled the needle through.

'Is it their feelings you're thinking of, I wonder, or your own?'

She went out of the room and left the question in the air.

Patience decided she had been frightened to go because she had feared embarrassment – her own. Excepting Doktor Meister – who was, after all, alive and perfectly well – she had never been in the presence of real tragedy. When grandparents had died she had been too young (they said) for funerals.

And when she did finally accept Laura's invitations, she found that she never knew what to expect. One day Mrs Meister would seem cheerful, almost normal, chattering on even more than usual, making a fuss of Patience; another, she would be lying in the dark, curtains drawn against the summer, dazed, dazzled, hardly hearing them, it appeared – then she would suddenly want something, a photograph, a letter, a book, and she must have it at once, now! And by the time they had found it she would want it no longer, forget why she ever asked for it. Quite pettishly, she complained: 'Why would I want that?' And then she would be contrite and, in an imitation of normality, sigh from her invalid couch: 'There is so much to do! How I'm ever going to get through the day, I really don't know. But Laura, my little Lolly, you are such a help and I'm so beastly to you.'

Another time, she mistook Patience for someone else and talked to her in a foreign language; then she beckoned, drew her down close to her and whispered in English: 'There are some sweeties in the tin in the corner cupboard. You may take two, because you are a dear sweet girl, but don't tell Lolly!' She put her fingers to her lips and with a strange, sly smile, confided: 'Don't you remember what lovely parties we had when Lolly didn't know?'

'Mrs Meister . . .'

'And the Countess! Those ridiculous feathers!' Laughing, Mrs Meister began to cough or choke – it was hard to tell which – and while Patience stood helpless, Laura reached for a small bottle of brownish-coloured liquid, poured a measure into a glass, added the same quantity of water and handed it to her mother. Sophy Meister was quiet then, and soon she slept.

In the kitchen, Laura said: 'I shouldn't have asked you to come. But she's all right sometimes.'

'Don't be silly. But she isn't well, is she? What was that brown stuff? Will it help?'

Laura shrugged. 'A sort of cough mixture. She used to take morphine, you see, and now she can't get it. That has some sort of drug in it – opium, I think. It makes her quieter. I try to trick her and make weaker each time, but when I'm not here she can get as much as she likes, of course. And now with Heini and Papa . . . At first she seemed numb. That went on for quite a long time after the news about Heini. Then she got like this. I had the doctor in once but she says he's a spy. I talked to him. At least I tried to.'

'Did you tell him about Heini?'

Laura shook her head. 'I couldn't. That was silly, I suppose.'

They took their tea up to Laura's tower room. It was dusk, a perfect summer evening. Laura stretched out on the bed, Patience too, gazing at the ceiling that reflected the peppery green of the lime tree in the street below.

'Is she mad?'

'The doctor says not quite. I don't know.'

There was Laura's hair and her skin, so close. They were whispering. Patience turned her face towards Laura's.

'You'll have to tell your father. About Heini, I mean.'

'He won't talk about Heini.' They lay in silence for a while.

'D'you like Jack Cardington?'

'He's an idiot.'

'Stephen Marlowe?'

'They're just boys.'

'Will you get married?'

'If I'm suited, as Scotty used to say.'

'I'll come with you, if you like, to tell your father.'

'I know you will.'

'What d'you think sex is really like? I don't mean the stuff they talk at school. I think it would be like being friends, only more so.'

Laura sat up, grinned. She pushed back her hair and yawned.

'I think it will be *quite* different.'

'I've never even been kissed. Have you?'

'Oh yes!' And Laura was suddenly above her, laughing, teasing Patience, the mad world shut out.

'Who?'

Patti lay back again.

'A boy – a friend of Heini's at Christmas in a cupboard. I'm not

95

even sure who it was because we were playing sardines in the dark and a lot of other people came in. And then there was Scotty.'

'Oh, I don't mean *women*.'

'It wasn't like women, actually. It was when we were dancing to the gramophone in Paris and Scotty just held me a little bit longer and kissed me like a man would. Like I think a real man would. If Maman had known she'd have sacked her, but Scotty didn't seem to care. It was only once.'

'But didn't you feel *awful*? Wasn't it absolutely horrible?'

'No. I just forgot about it till now. There are women like that, Patti. Scotty explained to me. I think they're often lonely.'

Patience shuddered. She was aware of the back of her hand and Laura's, almost touching. She remembered the brush of Laura's kiss, the night of the play.

'I think I'd better go now.'

At the door, Laura said: 'I'm sorry about my mother. But Heini was special to her always, you know. And I loved him too.' The strange little frisson of excitement, or fear, or foreboding that Patience had felt was gone. Laura looked so disconsolate and weary, quite ordinary, that Patience reached out and awkwardly the two girls embraced, simply and briefly, as friends.

So now Stalin was Uncle Joe – a matter of minimal interest to the girls who were living at the time in the twelfth century with Miss Trott. Trotty was clearly in love with Peter Abelard, of whom she spoke wistfully, especially after his castration. For sixpence, Barbara Baxter, with her medical background, explained the mechanics of poor Peter's loss.

'And thus,' declaimed Miss Trott, 'spiritual love drove out the merely carnal. Yes, Nina?'

'I was thinking about Heloise. It must have been frightful for her.'

'On the contrary. You will find as you grow up, Nina, that there are many kinds of love.'

Nina nibbled a nasturtium seed and pulled a face. 'I shouldn't think anyone ever loved Trotty, would you? Except old Winterboots in her fashion – and she seems to have gone off her. They're not as thick as they used to be. That's rather sad.'

Rose sighed. 'Perhaps she had a great love who was lost in the last war. Lots of people did. Almost all the men died.'

Patience kept her counsel. She had just made up her mind that, come what may, she wanted to be kissed by a man this summer – well, a boy she supposed, but it would have to be properly. It suddenly seemed very urgent, like swotting for an exam. Perhaps something would happen at farming camp? She considered the candidates, several of whom were sprawled in the shrubbery. Jack Cardington would kiss anybody. She'd rather it were Stephen, but he was so shy: how could she let him know she wanted to be kissed?

Kinds of love? What was love, anyway? Nina and her swains? Mrs Meister going mad for her son and her husband? Her mother and her father, talking quietly like birds on a branch, not touching much? Rosie's sunset view of happy-ever-after and then a nice funeral? Or Laura's Scotty. That must be fearful. Patti's mind approached the idea and slid away, not even to imagine. It would surely be terrible to be a woman like that.

The Carl Rosa were there for only one night, and Laura couldn't come so Patience didn't go either. Because she couldn't bear to go with the school, to share, even with the Lowrie crowd, *her* opera. She often felt that, about opera and music and plays, books too: if she loved them, they belonged exclusively to her, she wanted no one else's opinion, even their fervour. Her father used to tease her about this and that was the one time Patience did not like him; as for her mother – she had her painting, and that was hers.

There was someone they called the Fox in the desert now where her father was. Letters were always out of date and censored. Her father made jokes about sandwiches. The war down there did not seem to be going frightfully well. Patience wrote to him that they were going to the farming camp in Lincolnshire to single beet, and it might be quite fun. She said she had a new friend at school, 'a sort of refugee', but that seemed rather pointless: if she told him properly about Laura she might worry him – the letter might even be censored, though Patience didn't know if they blue-pencilled the ones going out as well as coming in. When she had first written to her father Patience had always made declarations of how much she missed him, longed for his return; but it was odd – she found it more and more difficult to remember him, she thought of the time she couldn't bear his going away as a kind of childhood. Often now, she did not give him a thought for days on end and the photograph of him in the lounge seemed the picture of a stranger. Did her mother feel the same? Patience did not know and would never have dreamed of asking. These two were English, the mother and daughter in the house in Spring Gardens. They spoke of the mechanics of life, of trivia, of necessities; passion, longing, anger, love – they must have had house-room, but they were folded away in clean drawers, confided to pillows, on waking nights, reduced to shadows behind a closing door.

The girls in the train bowled through the green fields. *Julia loved the blue sky and the broad fields, the calm oxen delight the eyes of the little girl. Where are the white roses of the cottage?*

They had the carriage to themselves and Laura let down the window and secured the strap.

'This is just how I thought England was,' she said. 'Look at that village – those pretty houses. It's heavenly!' Laura thought of that winter England, that had been so horrible, as a dark room. It was still there. She would return to it. But meanwhile.

Patience asked: 'Will your mother really be all right?'

Laura drew in her head. 'Oh, Lord, now I'll have smuts on my face. Yes, the doctor's given her some other stuff – chloral I think, so she's sleeping better. And there's always the old thing downstairs who said she'd pop in. It took ages to get to know her because every time we met her she pointed to her mouth and grinned and shook her head, so we thought she was loopy. But it turned out she just couldn't speak English so she and my mother natter away in a sort of Italian-French – she's really Hungarian and even Maman can't manage that. We call her Olga the Boots because she always wears Wellingtons, indoors and out. But she's really a Princess, or something. But, you see, that means I might be able to come to farming camp, if Maman goes on getting better!'

'That's marvellous.' Patience thought, Laura's too bright, she's talking too much, like her mother when she's a little bit mad. But Laura's not mad, she's frightened. She's frightened to tell her father about Heini.

Doktor Meister had been moved south, and though he claimed his conditions were much improved, it had been even more difficult to get visitors' passes. And they had to show them twice at two gates on the way up the gravel drive.

He was standing on a mown and rolled English lawn, risen from a deck-chair, with a newspaper under his arm, and Laura first hesitated, then called out, then running, called again: 'Papa!'

Patience hung back but then the doktor called for her to join them and the three circled the clipped lawn, visited the herbaceous border and the walled kitchen garden. Patience thought at first that Laura had changed her mind about mentioning Heini: she seemed still so gay, charged with brightness.

'So you see,' said the doktor, 'I lead the life of an idle English gentleman. Cabbages no more!'

They sat on a bench set against the kitchen garden wall. The wall faced south and a vine was trained against it. A gardener worked in the strawberry bed and beyond were the blue sleeping downs. Everything, Laura's father said, was done for him; he had a most comfortable room he would show them later, wireless, letters, papers: 'and even croquet! I have become quite a fiend at croquet.' He was still thin, too small for his clothes, Patience noticed, but his cuffs were no longer frayed. A little work, he said, yes, he did a little work, it would bore them – 'yet, you see, I enjoy it, it is a pleasure! They have found something useful in my poor old mind. So I am better. The brain, like the dog, needs exercise. And as for the body – these fields, as far as you can see, I am free to walk! And even old friends I meet here.'

The food was good too. Sometimes he felt like an ortolan, stuffed for eating.

How peculiar, though Patience, to be free and yet a prisoner. A prisoner and yet not a prisoner.

The doktor stood and slapped his pockets, for his pipe, thought better of it and remarked: 'The mind, you see, is always free. You would be surprised what goes on: we have our own string quartet – entirely professional – classes in every subject and every language you could imagine and a most ferocious chess club. 'You see that fellow there' – he indicated the stooped gardener – 'one of the world's greatest philosophers and he chooses to grow onions in his spare time! Some of the best minds in Europe here, all at this one house-party. We joke that if this place burned down, a large part of the world's culture would go with it.'

'But Papa, what do you *do*?'

'I do as I am told, my little Lolly. And I miss you.'

'Maman is sorry she couldn't come, but she's a bit better. I mean, she's quite all right, really, but the journey would be tiring.'

Doktor Meister nodded and the light had gone from Laura's face. They were walking now by the artificial lake, Laura had her arm through her father's, and Patience felt sorry for her. She had still not mentioned the purpose of her visit.

'You see,' said the doktor, 'they will understand the nonsense of this soon and then we will be together, a whole family again.'

Laura said, straight out, not looking at him: 'Papa, Heini has been posted missing.'

Nothing changed. In the English garden with the pretty lake, the flowers, the walls, the light, the light through the trees fragmenting their faces, sparking the lake where ducks dozed, one eye open. In the garden where deep in the shade a still statue was unmoved, there was nothing altered. Doktor Meister was expressionless, blank, even repeated, as though Laura had been talking gibberish.

'Heini? But I have no son?'

'Papa, you must understand. Heini may be dead.'

Then, without putting his hands to his face, without so much as a cry, he did weep, with the most terrible openness Patience had ever seen. 'Heini,' he said. 'Dead. *Tot*?' And though he made no movement he might have rent his garments and poured ashes on his head. 'But I have no son,' he said to the indifferent trees, 'so how can he be dead?' The sun continued to shine. The sky remained.

Patience, at first transfixed, strolled away from them to a bench nearby. She felt useless and embarrassed: in trying to support Laura she had wandered into a land of passion and feeling and tragedy – of love too – far beyond her experience. *Tot*: what a terrible word, worse even than dead or *mort*, three letters, one cold syllable like a heavy door slamming, a bolt being driven home, the stamp of an iron foot. Was the solemn boy in the photograph now one of death's trim men? Patience watched Laura and her father circle the lake. He walked fast, head bowed, and Laura had difficulty keeping up with him. She caught his elbow, they stopped and seemed to be talking vehemently, Laura insisting, then appearing to give up, a slump of despair.

By the time they had circled the lake and come back again to Patience, they had composed themselves. Doktor Meister even tried to make a joke, though it did not seem very funny.

'My daughter here, Miss Patience, tells me I am living in the past, I am a prisoner of the past, I must forgive. Grieving is not enough, I must recognise and absolve.' Now he was not being at all funny, though he was smiling as people do when they make a joke, and Patience was wishing that she did not have the kind of face even adults, even strangers, confided in.

They were walking back to the house, past an area of Nissen huts, contained – like the Arboretum camp – within a double row of high fences of meshed wire, crowned by barbed wire. All that was missing was the watchtower. Was the fence to keep people in or to keep them out? A prison within a prison? This place was very puzzling.

'What's in there, Papa?'

The doktor wagged his finger. 'Now that, Princess Lolly, is *verboten*. For you to enter, for me to speak of.' His mood had lifted a little and he paused to light his pipe, pressing down the tobacco in the bowl, turning away from the breeze that had come up.

'Do you work there?'

'Sometimes, when I need to give my mind a run. At the moment I am deciding. It is tempting. It would be better for all of us: for the family, I mean. I would still be here, but there would be privileges; I could help your mother in little ways – money perhaps, a better flat.'

'But you couldn't come home?'

'Alas, no.' He shook his head. 'Let us say I would be a guest rather than a prisoner of His Majesty's government.'

Laura was confused, close to tears. 'But Papa, I don't understand!'

Her father put a forefinger under her chin and raised it very gently 'And I must not explain because I must not. My poor Lolly, you bear the brunt. This is a mad time. We must think of it as an illness. It will pass, we will be together again. We will be well. And now you must be off before the guard dogs eat you!'

Now Laura flung herself into his arms and they were talking in German and French, kissing, hugging.

Patience felt, as she had feared she would, a gooseberry. 'Laura, I do think we'd better go. Or we'll miss the train.'

On the interminable journey back north – at least, unlike that other passage, it was made not in darkness but summer evening and then dusk, and they had a carriage to themselves – the two girls spoke hardly at all. It was the same country through which they returned, still pretty, the same smiling cottages, but this time this soft England seemed artificial, a stage set, an illusion. Laura sat, leaning back in the corner seat, not seeing the view from the window, not drawn.

At last Patience asked: 'What exactly does your father *do*? I mean, I know he's clever but you've never said.'

Though her eyes were open, Laura seemed to have to wake to turn to Patience and answer her. 'He's what they call a doktor, and a professor. That is, there are about four people in the world who know as much as he does about philosophy and physics. And only one other who knows about both. Unless you count Bertrand Russell, but he's mathematics really.'

'I've heard of him. D'you know him?'

'He tried to have a flirt with my mother. But she said he looked like a gerbil and hadn't the faintest idea how to handle women. I think they're asking my father to do something he doesn't want to do. I'm sorry I dragged you into all this.'

'It sounds horrible. Like keeping an animal fed in a cage to make him do tricks. But I didn't mind coming. I just wondered if you should have been private.'

Laura leaned forward, across the carriage, and took Patience's hand in hers.

'But Patti, dear Patti, I simply couldn't have managed without you! Don't you realise? That you were my first friend in England that horrible time when it was winter and I was wearing all the wrong clothes. And you were nice to me. Really only you and Miss Trott. And you will always be my friend, anywhere.'

Patience took a deep breath. 'You were right about Trotty. I never told you, she doesn't want us to be friends. It was horrible. I felt sick for days.'

First Laura was open-mouthed with astonishment, then she began to laugh. She waved a hand, a queen dismissing an inadequate courtier. 'Then pouf! to Trotty. She can go. We don't need her. Goodbye, Miss Trott, you may leave the stage.'

'You honestly don't mind?'

Laura sat back. 'You know, since the play, and Heini and everything – it all seems muddled up – and that stuff they wrote about me, I've decided not to care what anyone thinks of me. Except you, of course, and my father. And Scotty perhaps, if I knew where she was.' Then she sobered again, her face closed as it did sometimes when her mother was there and when she first saw those awful words and the sign on her desk. And other times when for no reason Patience understood, Laura went miles away from her into some dark land. 'And Heini,' she said. 'I would mind about Heini.'

They were entering the industrial Midlands. Factories now, mills, the black pit-wheels and tips.

'You know,' said Laura. 'That old Jew in the *Marché des Puces*, he used to keep a *serin* – a canary you call it – a bird with yellow feathers in a wooden cage. One day he said he would let it free but Scotty said it would never survive for more than a day. Yet all the time it used to peck your finger and try to get out.'

The coal screes, then the marshalling yard, the slow crawl into the station, the train in the siding, bored soldiers calling, headed south. The black lump of the castle.

They were home. It was dark.

9

Thumping through flat Lincolnshire in a lorry, singing and being silly, with their tin mugs tied to their rucksacks and the world all green. A good spell, mist on the fields in the morning when Patience and Rose Delane crept out early to paddle in the dew, and were startled by a herd of cows they heard before they saw: the soft, wet tug of their grazing, very close; Rose gasped for a moment with fright, then the herd emerged from the white air, still wearing scarves of mist. The cows, long-lashed and short-sighted, looked at the girls, the girls at the cows. Rose whispered: 'Look at their breath, you can see it. Will they chase us?' 'They're only cows,' said Patience. 'Come on, I'm hungry.'

They were always hungry at the camp. Ravenous with health. One day in the fields Posy Potter ate a raw potato and was sick. They were singling beet, up and down, up and down. *Julia is a farmer's daughter/We are daughters of Britain.* In the next field the boys worked, stripped off their shirts as the noon sun rose. When it rained they met under a hedge at lunch break and had snail races.

They never ate with the prisoners. The prisoners were sent to a barn.

Breakfast, queuing at the hatch and the clatter of tin plates on wooden table, the scrape of chairs. Whoever was Mum today stayed behind with one other to wash up and peel spuds, clean and cook. Groans. But you got a bit extra that way: bread and dripping for elevenses and sometimes cheese.

'Rotten about Laura,' said Jack Cardington, looking quite different in the country, rather nicer. Sprawled against a haystack taking the odds on snails.

Patience said: 'She couldn't leave her other with Olga the Boots for more than a week. But she'll be here on Monday.'

'Cheers.'

'Watch it. Here comes hockey-stick.'

'Barbara's not so bad. She's better here.'

Stephen Marlowe and Patience sat a little apart from the others. They swopped paste sandwiches and Spam. Patience thought sometimes Stephen gave her more than her fair share. He was nice. He said, 'It's *Pimpernel Smith* next week in the flea-pit. You going?'

'Leslie Howard!' Nina rolled her eyes.

'I don't know if they'd let us.'

'What are you doing?' Barbara wanted to know.

'Racing snails,' said Jack. 'D'you want one? I've got quite a stable. You can have my second runner.'

'No thanks. I'll watch.'

Posy asked Patience: 'D'you think Belle Isolde is a silly name for a snail?'

They worked up the row, down the row. Rose told them stories to keep them going, mostly about Ireland and funerals, though some were love stories and they were sad too. Patience looked up, stretching her back, and Stephen waved from the next field. She was not certain if he had asked her to go with him to the film, which would be quite different to just going anyway. She hoped he had. She wondered if they would let them go.

They were Miss Mallard and Miss Lowrie who were in charge of the girls' camp. Well, hardly a camp really, more of a house; a rather grand one, too, handed over or requisitioned for the duration. Mallard sometimes came down and worked in the fields with the girls, which spoiled the fun. Miss Lowrie, to Rose's ravishment, wore sprigged cotton and a soft straw hat tied under the chin, like one of Marie Antoinette's dairy-maids. In sandals, carrying a basket, she sought out the brown new-laid eggs that nestled in farmyard secret places and hedgerows. From the neglected herbaceous border she plucked flowers for the rough table. And on a fine day, her duties done, would be found by the girls when they returned, reading in a hammock between trees. There she lay curled – much as she did in the staffroom window-seat; but from here, this garden, Violetta Lowrie could see the view she had often dreamed of. Though, of course, it was not hers, or only on loan. When Josephine Mallard stomped into her field of vision, Miss Lowrie unfocused her eyes slightly until the games mistress hardly existed at all, poor soul.

'Lowrie says we can go to the pictures!' said Nina.
'What about Mallard?'
'Didn't ask.'

'Alouette! Gentille Alouette! Alouette, je te plumerai.'
It was only in the evenings that they travelled with the prisoners, who started work an hour earlier in the morning, and whose camp lay halfway between the girls' hostel and the farm.

They were Italian, not at all the same as the Germans in the Arboretum. In the first place, they were let out to work. And then – so they said in the mangled French that seemed the only common language – they hated indiscriminately Musso, Churchill, Roosevelt and Hitler. After all Miss Winterton's sermons about not consorting with the enemy, it seemed strange to be bundled into one lorry with them, to talk, to sing silly French songs with these brown-eyed, jolly young men who said they had never wanted to fight anyone anyway.

'English,' they said,'OK. *Les Allemands* stink.'
The girls giggled. They brought them apples, the Eyties smuggled in a bottle of some funny home-made drink. One linked arms with Nina, who didn't mind, and the songs became rather rude.

Auprès de ma blonde, qu'il fait bon, fait bon, fait bon, auprès de ma blonde, qu'il fait bon dormir!
Through the villages they rocked in their singing lorry, crammed to bursting. Even Barbara Baxter singing and every time the lorry lurched the cottage gardens and the hedgerows tipped. Those long, straight Roman roads between flatness and flatness heaved like hills.

Fortunately, it was Mallard's night off.
Miss Lowrie said she would draw a veil over the whole thing but someone must see to Posy, who was going to be sick.

A social, it was called, on the Saturday night, and everyone was supposed to dress up. Mallard left and Mam'selle arrived, just in time to play the piano. Rose wound flowers in her hair, either as Ophelia or the Lady of Shalott; Barbara wore a Hitler moustache made of charcoal. Most of the boys arrived as Caesar or Arab sheiks. Patience could not think of anything. Flowers did not suit her. Cordelia King was Britannia. Miss Lowrie lent Patience her dairy-maid hat and found her a long white frilled apron, which they washed and starched in Robin starch: 'There we are!' cried Miss Lowrie, 'A Watteau rustic!'

Patience did not know what a Watteau rustic was but it was better than going as nothing at all, and Stephen said she looked nice.

He said he couldn't be a sheik because of the colour of his hair, so he'd better be Lawrence of Arabia. They danced and ate baked potatoes and walked in the tangled garden where in the dusk everything white shone and there were spikes of scent from tobacco plants and white fleshy lilies; if you bent to smell the lilies, they left a powdering of saffron on your nose.

Patience, happy, had the same sense of tension she had felt when, leaning from her bedroom window, she had seen the orchard in the Manifold Valley as a stage. This time though, it was darker and more beautiful, like a garden in Chekhov. The drawing-room windows were open and the shutters not closed, so after blackout Mam'selle had to play by touch in the dark. When they read *The Cherry Orchard* in class, Miss Lowrie said it was a comedy to make you cry. There seemed no barrier between the garden and the drawing-room, they flowed one into the other and people walked in and out. Stephen bent to blow the yellow lily dust from Patience's cheek and his lips touched her cheek although all he was doing was blowing away the yellow dust – surely that was all he was doing? Patience could hardly breathe for the sensation of the white-robed figure who was and was not Stephen, his face so close now he too had that pollen on his cheek. The ghosts of sheep grazed on the other side of the ha-ha and there was Nina, a wanton shepherdess. Then there was a cry from inside the house, the music stopped and Mam'selle cried out. Mam'selle, transported into her native language, cried: '*Elle est arrivée!*'

Once Laura arrived it was different. Better and worse. The weather changed and settled into a dry hot spell. They worked slowly, pausing for a rest at the end of each row. Cordelia King got sunstroke and had to lie in the dark in the sixth-form dormitory. Mam'selle read her *Le Grand Meaulnes* in French until Cordelia pretended to sleep. Pearls before pigs, sighed Mam'selle. Swine, said Miss Lowrie, vaguely and automatically, out of school-teaching habit.

'Why Moan, anyway?' said Nina as they lay in the dark, too hot to sleep.

'*Meaulnes*,' said Laura.

'What's it about?'

'A place of perfect happiness you went to once, and are always trying to find again.'

'Did you know if you take a single strand of your hair and run it between your finger and your thumb, and it curls, that means you're a flirt?'

Barbara groaned: 'Nina, some of us want to go to sleep.'

Patience whispered: 'I'm so glad you've come.'

'So am I,' said Laura. 'This is like that book. A place of perfect happiness.'

'It's jolly hard work.'

They sat under the hedge. It did not rain. The snails were sluggish and disinclined to race. In this wide country of low sky you could see the curve of the earth but at midday even that melted and was marked only by puffs of dust as a car passed, or a cart. The field they had half-worked shimmered and danced, the sky was white. The Eyties were marched off to their barn to eat, and the girls waved. It was hard to think of them as prisoners, enemies. A solitary, harmless little Tiger Moth crossed the sky very slowly, out for a stroll. This was a pocket of time, out of the war, just as it was time stolen from school. Once, when things were bad, Patience thought that life might be a series of cages: childhood in the playpen, men behind wire, school, work, marriage perhaps (though that was not something she envisaged for herself), home, love, anger. And the hardest cage of all might be life itself. You might struggle from one cage, only to find yourself in another. In spite of Doktor Meister's *tot* – that syllable hard as a stone – she was still too young to envisage death as more than a door slammed in your face.

The boys came over from their field with a bottle of precious Tizer. Stephen's face was as brown now, almost, as the Italians', and his hair bleached like Heini's. Patience moved up to make room for him, but he settled next to Laura. The bottle was passed along with the respectful awe and care given to communion wine. Patience dozed. When she woke, Nina was tugging her arm: 'Come on, fathead, Laura and Stephen have found a pool.'

Patience looked at her watch. 'We can't. We've got to get back to work.' In Cordelia's absence, she and Barbara were senior prefects, in charge of the work gang.

'Barbara's gone too – it's marvellous. The cows can't get there because of the wood. It's very deep and cold.'

Laura and Stephen.

'I don't care,' said Nina, 'I'm going in starkers!' She stripped down to bra and pants and plunged in. Laura and Stephen sat on the opposite bank, side by side, dabbling their feet. The water both lit and dimmed their faces, green and a wavering gold.

Stephen took Laura to see Leslie Howard.

'He's rather sweet, isn't he?'

'Stephen Marlowe or Leslie Howard?'

'Don't be an idiot,' said Nina. 'You know I always fancy older men.' Nina put down the mirror and looked at Patience. 'I say, you're not upset are you that Laura's pinched Stephen?'

'Of course not. There was nothing to pinch anyway.'

'Then that's all right. Just wondered. You're a funny old fish, Patti.'

They came back in September for the potato picking, and this was one of the best times of all. The Boys' High weren't there but the Italians were and Patience and the rest, recently elevated to the sixth, slept on mattresses instead of palliasses. And then there was the hay, and the harvest, and the molten light, cider apples, orchards. There was the harvest festival in Church and the girls and the prisoners were allowed to ride there together, all on one cart drawn by two drays with flowers in their harness. Piled on the cart were the offerings of potatoes, marrows, apples, bursting plums. Children threw flowers at the cart, a few cottage daisies and the last of the wild honeysuckle. The Church bells were silent, would ring only for victory or invasion, but everyone sang that harvest night riding through the dusk, in any language known to them. At one moment, when the cart lurched, Laura clasped Patience's wrist but, as though the tower of Babel had fallen down – for the sound was of one voice – still they went on singing.

10

And now they too were ranked among the glorious. Lower Sixth certainly but angels nonetheless, possessed of both duties and privileges. Patience and Barbara, for instance, were now fully-fledged prefects with the right to inflict punishment of their choice without reference to higher authority. (Though it was understood that such retribution should not be corporal. Rather an irony that, Lucy Trott thought more than once, considering the physical violence that went on, to which one turned a blind eye, provided blood was not drawn. And that was human nature, in a boys' school, a girls' school, in the world. What was war but legalised violence? She had brought this up once with Claire, when they had been close.)

They had the right to the sixth-form study and – in theory at least – to wear rather gorgeous red cloaks instead of navy gaberdine: one of Miss Winterton's wilder flights of fancy that used to produce yearly thirty or so Little Red Riding Hoods, till red went for army nursing blankets, because it was the colour of blood. Now the cloaks were grey and of an inferior material, often home-made. Patience stuck to her gaberdine raincoat, Nina fastened her cloak at the throat with a red ribbon (strictly against the rules – though, as Nina said, no one had ever laid down a rule, so, as far as she was concerned, no rule existed). Rose wore hers because it made her look like a nurse but only Laura wore it with an air.

Cordelia King (of course) was this year's Head Girl. Very stately she was, carrying her badge – a white tin shield as distinct from the prefects' little bar – as though to office born. She had given up RADA in favour of Oxford, or Cambridge at the least. Pooh, said Nina, she's training to be queen.

'And next year it'll be Baa-baa Baxter, you see,' groaned Nina. The usual crowd, preferring still the boiler-room to the sixth-form study where Lady Cordelia frowned if you smoked, considered the prospect in silence for a while.

Rose said: 'She was nicer at camp?'

'Camp was different.'

'People don't change.'

Old Bill was tapping the pipes somewhere. Nina thought he did it to annoy. The boiler growled.

'That thing'll blow up one day.'

Rose pondered. 'I wonder why Barbara's so horrid? I mean she couldn't have been *born* like that. Babies are lovely.'

Nina hooted and flung her arm round Rose's shoulder: 'Oh, Rosie, you are the sweetest! If all the world were you, we'd be all right.' And then: 'But it doesn't have to be bloody Baxter, you know. Patience – you could be Head Girl. We'd all vote for you.'

'Oh no!' Patience thought. 'No, I wouldn't like that a bit.'

'Why not?'

'I don't know. I think I wouldn't like people looking at me. And Them. I'd feel I belonged to Them. I couldn't come down here any more.'

The others nodded glumly. 'Oh Lord, I'm sick of school,' said Nina.

'But d'you think it's better outside?' said Patience.

'That's a funny thing to say.'

'Yes, it is. I've only just thought that lately.'

The bell went. Walking back to the classroom, Nina hung back with Patience.

'Where was Laura today? Now Barbara's stopped, she could come anytime. Is she having a mad affair with Stephen Marlowe?'

'I don't know,' said Patience.

Now the trees were nearly leafless, Lucy Trott could see from the Head's study across the camp into the Arboretum as far as the abandoned summer-house, set just where two paths met, each leading to a different gate in Albert Road. Here she spied two figures, one a girl and the other a boy, part and take their separate paths. The girl in her grey cloak ran. Miss Trott noted their identities but said nothing to Miss Winterton. She would wait to see what use, if any, she might make of this information. Lately, she had been left to resume her night prowls of the school in peace, for her fire-watching partner now was the little Frenchwoman, who dozed off every night over her knitting, leaving Lucy free.

As for Claire, Lucy tried not to think of that: how hurtful of her to go off alone to Matlock – if, indeed, she had been alone. While Lucy herself spent a most uncomfortable fortnight in a Yorkshire guest-house.

'I'm sorry, Claire, what did you say?'

'I have been wondering,' said the Head, 'whether we should reconsider the election system for Head Girl.'

'It seems to work well enough?'

Claire adjusted the grey silk cravat she had taken to wearing and smiled with the greatest and vaguest sweetness.

'What I wonder, Lucy, is are the masses, so to speak, capable of coming to a mature decision for the good of all? Are we asking too much of them?'

No reply was expected. Claire's questions, lately, had become increasingly rhetorical.

Lucy concluded the school business they had between them and left the study with a strange sense of having her own words returned to her. How often she had recommended to Claire the merits of benevolent dictatorship. But at least to preserve the semblances of democracy . . . Miss Trott wagged her head and a new girl wondered who was the funny old thing in the baggy grey cardigan with the wispy hair, talking to herself.

Patience did not know if Laura and Stephen were having a mad affair. She wasn't even sure what a mad affair was, and had hardly seen Laura properly since the new term began. She went straight home after school every day. She and her mother talked only of necessary things though one night she thought she heard her mother crying, as people do into pillows. Once, when Mary Mackenzie was out, Patience found the sketches of the Manifold Valley pushed away in the bottom drawer of her father's desk. The watercolours were quite good, but the best was a quick pastel sketch done on the hill above the valley, of two girls, one lying, one sitting up with her arms round her knees – herself and Laura. To Patience that summer seemed now as far away as a country she had visited when she was very young and to which she would never return. And her vow that this summer she would be kissed, properly? Well, perhaps Stephen's lips had brushed her cheek.

Then one day going home she heard feet running after her. It was a November afternoon, one of those days when the wind ripped the sky to rags of flying colour from palest milk-blue to purple and you either scurried, head bent, or walked boldly into it; leaves, scraps of newspaper, dust, whirled around Laura and the hood of her grey cape was blown back, her cheeks pink as she caught up with Patience. She was smiling. Her hair was wild. She was happy.

'You've been avoiding me. But now, you see, I've caught you. You must come for tea now! Everything is *good*, Patti – I've so much to tell you!'

The Meisters' flat had always been for Patience a place of enchantment; sometimes magical, sometimes cursed – but entering it, she never failed to feel the otherness of the Meisters' world in those dark and cluttered rooms. As though she crossed a frontier into a foreign country.

And now here was Olga the Boots from the basement – wearing, indeed, Wellington boots, also a kerchief knotted at the back of her head, a long black skirt; and she smiled, chattered, for Patience spoke a word of French or English, then tumbled into incomprehension but smiled away like the picture of a happy Russian peasant in a fairy tale. Nodding and winking in some sign language for Patience's benefit, she conveyed welcome and laid out the girls' tea. Another tray she carried down the corridor to Mrs Meister's boudoir-sitting-room. And from here came violent shouts of rage and quarrel.

Laura laughed: 'It's all right, really. They love to fight. They throw china sometimes. It's good for my mother – you know, like masters and servants used to fight in those Russian plays. Well, that's how it did happen, when they were young! When they were both children. Olga bullies her like her old nurse and Maman yells back. Come on, let's take tea to my room.'

It wasn't the same in the tower bedroom, yet nothing in the room had changed.

Laura sat before the dressing-table, brushing her crackling hair. Everything was better, truly, Olga was so good with Maman and then the doktor had taken that job, whatever it was. He couldn't come home but they could see him as often as they liked and there was more money, a lovely room, he could write, read, go as far as the village.

'I can't stay long, Laura. I'm terribly glad about your father.'

Patience lay back on Laura's bed, arms stiff as a soldier's by her sides. She looked at the ceiling. And she heard Laura say: 'And, Patti, the best of it is: I'm in love!'

'With Stephen Marlowe?'

'Yes. How *did* you guess? He's so sweet, so kind . . . but we'll keep it a secret, please, for you and me?'

'For you and me and Stephen.'

'Well, of course. And he's so handsome. I think he's the most handsome boy I've ever met.'

Patience left then. She did not see Sophy Meister. At the door Laura seized her hands: 'A secret! You promise? I trust no one, Patti, but you. But I do love him.'

Patience wrote letters to her father because she could hardly remember him and he was in Libya in a place, she felt, beyond the reach of letters where wastes of emptiness became battlefields and she could not grasp them. But she wrote to the idea of him perhaps because he belonged to a childhood that lay now – even further than that summer in Derbyshire – impenetrable behind walls and brambles and briar hedges.

She wrote:

I feel so strange and that no one will love me. I shall never have an air like Laura, or pretty legs and hair like mother, so how could a boy or a man ever look at me? I used to think it would be different when I grew up and left school, but now that's not so far away and I believe it will be just the same. I look at couples on the bus or in the Arboretum, everywhere, and any man who isn't absolutely horrible is always with a pretty girl.

Do you remember, when I was small, you used to tell me I was the fairest of them all? Then I got old enough to know I wasn't but I didn't mind very much. I just thought I wouldn't get married so

I'd be a famous author or help people instead. Or be a teacher like Trotty (I've changed my mind about that – she used to terrify me and I admired her a bit, now she seems sometimes just a lonely old woman. She said something horrid to me once I can't even tell you. I don't hate her for it, but I don't like her any more).

All this would be very boring for you but I don't suppose I'll send this letter. I write a lot of letters to you and then tear them up or lock them in my private box. I think mother looks in my drawers and when she thinks I'm writing to you, she wants to know what I've said. So I pretend I'm doing homework.

Anyway, just lately I've started to mind very much and for a bad reason I'm ashamed of. There was a boy I liked and I thought he liked me or even a bit more. And now he's fallen in love with Laura, who is my best friend. And I realise he's probably been in love with her for a long time. I think it was he who sent her some flowers after the play. I told you about her. She's a refugee and has a difficult life, so it's even worse that I envy her.

Mother's calling, so I'd better go. She's found a man who sells us eggs, but he can only come after dark, like a smuggler. We're getting on all right and the raids aren't nearly so bad, so you're not to worry.

This is an awful letter, all about me. And who wants to read about that!

I'm locking this letter in my box now and putting the key in the secret place she doesn't know about. I'll probably tear it up or leave it in the box.

They ate at a card table in front of the fire, with the wireless on. Mary Mackenzie smiled once at the programme. They did not speak. They cleared away quickly, not to miss ITMA. Mary Mackenzie knitted. Patience did her homework and often her mother would put aside the knitting and read, sometimes for an hour or more – mostly travel books written before the war or novels set in foreign places. Not romances though. Patience wondered if her mother believed in romance. She had been – she still was – so pretty everyone told Patience her mother had swept her father off his feet. Somehow she could imagine her father doing the sweeping, but not her mother being swept. You never knew though. Sometimes the most sensible-seeming people concealed depths, like Rose's sister, the plain one, who was down for a nun and at the last moment ran off in the middle of the night with a Protestant insurance man.

Patience looked at the photograph of her father on the desk where she worked, then at the mirror by the desk that reflected her mother by the fire. Mary Mackenzie had let the book slip to her lap and sat, with the finger in the page she had reached, while she rested her cheek against the wing of the chair and gazed at the small fire. She did look older, after all: there was a line between her eyes which stayed now, even in respose, even when she smiled there was still that little frown.

She was reading a book by Norman Douglas, called *South Wind*.

For the first time Patience could imagine being as old as her mother. What frightened was not arriving there, but the years between – a path that seemed to her at this moment as obscure as a dull walk on a moonless night.

Another thought that passed through Patience's mind was that her mother did not wish to be where she was, but, like the prisoners in the camp, she had no choice.

Once, when Patience was about seven, she went on a seaside holiday with her parents, somewhere in the West Country. It was a fortnight of freak hot weather. Her mother sat on the rocks and painted pictures that the little girl thought were wonderful: the colours were so bright. She painted one especially for her daughter, that Patience kept until it was lost. One night Patience looked out of her bedroom window and saw a couple walking on the beach, arm in arm, very close. Then they stopped and kissed.

That was unusual. Her parents did not touch very often.

Under the red-shaded lamp Mary Mackenzie shifted as if she had been asleep, though her eyes had been open. For a moment she appeared almost startled to find where she was, just as people wake and for a second or two imagine themselves to be in some other bed than their own, or to be in their own when in fact they are travelling.

'Well,' said Mary Mackenzie, as though concluding a conversation. Then she went to make the Horlicks.

·   ·   ·

117

'Laura? Lolly!' The plaintive note reached to the kitchen where Laura was reading while the stew simmered. Her mother and Olga the Boots had had a falling-out, involving food thrown, so Laura had to cook and keep her mother company. Sighing, she put down her book. 'Lolly! Where are you?'

Laura stood at her mother's door. 'I'm bringing in supper soon, Maman.'

Sophy sank back on her cushions. 'My poor Lolly. It's too much for you. Tomorrow I'll cook! I'll go to the shops and I'll get a chicken and do a *cocotte bonne femme*.'

'We can't get chicken, Maman.'

'Oh well then, a *gratin*. This stupid rationing!'

'We've used up our cheese ration.'

'Well, potatoes? We have potatoes? That is, in any case, the true *gratin* – without cheese.'

'Did you want something, mother? You called.'

'I forget, I forget. I was thinking I was alone.'

Laura brought in the vegetable stew. She had never learned to cook and wished very much that Olga would come back. She forced herself to eat the midday meal at school – they called it dinner – to save rations at home; though she knew the larger helping she had given her mother would not be finished, and would have to be saved and served again tomorrow, in disguise. She wondered if it was that chloral stuff the doctor gave her mother, that took Sophy's appetite. Maman ought to get out more, she knew. She would be better if they could at least live in the village near Papa? But there was school. And now Laura had her own secret reason for staying.

After supper Laura washed up. Her mother was bright now, she wanted to talk – sometimes she almost missed that old *vache* from downstairs – she wanted her jewel box that Papa said should be in the bank but how could she? Each gem had a tale to tell and Laura remembered how, as a child, she had loved these stories of parties and beaux and travel and those long dead – the shining world before the war. But Sophy got muddled now, and Laura could not always be bothered to prompt her. She gave her mother her medicine and sat with a book till it worked. Sophy's *histoires* grew disjointed, blurred, her voice thickened, she dabbled her fingers in the jewels and talked still, eyes closed, like a tired nun telling her rosary.

('But why can't you come out?' said Stephen. 'Because I have to be with my mother.')

Laura looked at Sophy, sleeping now, the dark violet smudges beneath her eyes, her hair greying where she had applied the henna slapdash, the jewels tangled in her fingers. When she was small how she had loved her scented dancing mother, the touch of her cheek at night as Sophy kissed before she danced away. And her trailing green sleeves in a garden on a summer evening blown, then folding round Laura's shoulders like wings: but you must go, go sweetheart, nurse is waiting.

Scotty did not approve of her mother, Laura knew that. Scotty thought Sophy Meister was incompetent.

At first, Laura had thought her mother was a Princess.

Then she had wanted to kill her mother to have her father to herself. Once Heini had been sent away she had planned ways – a thin wire, for instance, across the stairs? – Laura the younger had said *oui, Maman, non, Maman, merci, Maman* with her eyes cast down and murder in her heart until she had burst with guilt and cried all over Scotty on an Alpine holiday. Scotty had said that was perfectly normal. She questioned Laura closely on matters that seemed unrelated to the present drama, then marched her down the mountain and bought her a packet of Kotex. It was eighteen months before Laura actually needed to open the packet and follow Scotty's brisk and remembered instructions, and by then she was on the boat-train from Paris when she went to the *lavabo*. Scotty had warned her it often happened first away from home and had packed the embarrassing parcel in the tapestry hold-all they carried on the journey. Laura wore the same towel that day and for the first three days in the hotel in London. She was shamed. She felt hurt and at the same time guilty for the hurt inflicted on her. After three days the flow stopped and Laura shredded the pad and put it down the hotel lavatory ignoring the receptacle provided. She watched her blood flow away and noticed that, ironically, the lavatory basin – very fine on its claw pedestal – was made in Dresden.

Sophy stirred in her sleep and muttered, her jaw slack.

Scotty had said: 'Your mother will always find someone to look after her.'

And now, for the time at least, Laura was her mother's mother.

119

She tried to take away the jewel box but the beads and brooches and gems could not be prized from Sophy's fingers without waking her. Laura turned out the light.

He was waiting and they walked up and down the quiet street, thankful for blackout. All the same they whispered.

'I could come in?'

'No,' she said. 'Olga the Boots hears all.'

'We must find somewhere.'

'Yes.'

They kissed. They never did talk very much. Stephen touched her breast under her cloak. They were shy and ravenous.

'You're shivering.' He took off his coat and warmed her in it. Laura was reminded of her mother's green sleeves, folded round her shoulders, like wings.

Something was brewing. Some violence. The trees shook. The rooks warned. Stephen Marlowe – no longer the boy in cricket whites running out of the sun – was tackled on the pitch and fell, lay one second too long, his face in the mud, gaze turned to the crazy whirling turrets of Albert Lodge; and was kicked in the head. He stood. Blood ran in his eye. On the other side of the fence the prisoners walked in mud – their huts were raised above it; they walked in small groups, or singly, hands shoved deep in their pockets. They did not look out very much, at this time of year, their senses were dulled, the moving picture outside too familiar perhaps, or too painful in its ordinariness. They had turned in on themselves by now, made their own community, their city, their state; to survive. One or two suffered for this necessary survival, became prisoners within a state within a prison. At this time of year with the trees leafless, they felt exposed, though they had become by now such a feature of the landscape people rarely gave them a glance. From the beginning, many had hurried their children past, or turned away, as if from an indecency, then snatched a quick, covert look. (Heini, if he were not dead, could be in a place like this.)

One behind the fence – a boy in a greatcoat and scarf but no cap, with hair cut so short to his scalp it looked grey, or it was grey – watched Stephen. He grinned and tapped his head where Stephen's blood flowed. He might have been friendly.

Jack Cardington came up beside Stephen. 'I say, you are a mess.' He jerked his head in the direction of the camp. 'Ought to give them a game sometime, poor sods. Not on though, I suppose, bloody Jerries. Not like the Eyties, are they? Not jolly chaps.'

Stephen ducked his head under the stinging shower – rationed for victory – and gasping, was on the edge of an illumination. Something to do with victims, with strangeness, with blood. Brilliance? Something to do with Laura. He pressed the towel to his forehead but still the blood flowed. He would have died for Laura.

Tension, like orders, come from above.

A scene, previously peaceful, can (as Stephen discovered when kicked in the head) shift, dissolve, shudder, re-form, stripped trees become men, rain, blood.

Everyone was snappish in the staffroom – time of year. Mam'selle's cat-like sneezes irritated, there was an air of fatigue, coffee-cup rings on the table, cigarette burns in the rug, stained and torn upholstery that would not be renewed. Lucy Trott brooded. Lowrie was wearing lipstick, Mallard sat with her legs apart. Several new faces this year and none welcome. Someone knocked over someone else's exercise books. Marking. Would there be no end to marking? Women together. Time of year, time of war.

Claire had announced that after consultation with the governors there would be no more elections. Barbara Baxter would be next year's Head Girl.

Oh, thought Lucy, to be quietly beneath a vine with Hadrian. Failing Claire. *Animula vagula, blandula, hospes comesque coporis.* Not that she and Claire had ever . . . An Emperor unsuitable for girlish minds. Claire had been so cold yet with whom but Lucy had she shared – could she ever share – those violet shades, the clear light of Pericles, tea brewed on their travelling primus where Xerxes once sat. No golden thrones for Mallard, nor the tumbling hills of Corinth: she'd seen them, the Mallards, stomping round Baedeker with rucksacks without books.

Claire had lost her balance a little, but to be dismissed so coldly!

Lucy Trott slashed through in red an incorrect subjunctive, closed the last exercise book, straightened her skirt and stood up just as the bell rang. She felt better. She had made up her mind to give Claire what she wanted: the German girl.

At the same moment there was a fierce and unsanctioned clash between the smaller followers of the aesthetes and those of the hearties. Patience, playground prefect for the day, whistle to her lips, watched in horror as one lower-school soldier fell from the Arboretum terrace wall onto the spiked railings and was, for one eternal moment, impaled.

Not as bad as it might have been, whatever the rooks cried as they rose at the scream from the playground and in the air repeated it: Ware, Ware! Then silence, in the sky and on the earth, a grey hush of shock. Even a few of the prisoners had noticed and the boy with the shaved head clutched the fence.

It was only half a minute and Patience grabbed the nearest of the small ones:

'Fetch matron. And tell Miss Trott. Tell her we need an ambulance. Hurry!'

Not so bad. Her arm slashed but her cardigan had caught her. Shocked, of course. Off to hospital with her and right as rain tomorrow. Run away, little girls! Miss Trott waved her hand. She was pleased with Patience, who had behaved sensibly. Perhaps that little talk of theirs had had some effect? Certainly she hadn't seen her around so much with the German girl. Looked peaky though. Ah well, puberty, war and winter.

'I do think, Patience my dear,' said Miss Trott, 'that we should consider extra tutorials if we are to get you to Oxford. Mr Hitler permitting, of course.'

Ware! said the rooks. Ugly birds.

II

After the incident of the impaling Miss Winterton announced that there was to be a tightening-up. Miss Trott nodded. Divisive and hysterical elements would be dealt with sharply.

Violetta Lowrie looked down at her trim ankles.

Josephine Mallard glared ahead as though ready to shoot the first dissenter.

Mam'selle sniffed.

There was a boiler-room debate.

Posy couldn't think what they meant.

'Pashes, I suppose,' said Nina, with contempt. 'You know. Little girls running after big girls, like Rose and Miss Lowrie.' Nina was getting the curse and felt less than usually charitable.

'Nina!' Rose was as near to angry as she might ever be, but she blushed. 'Anyway, she meant the lower school. And it's Barbara's fault, she encourages it. It's funny, she used to be nice. What do you think, Laura?'

'I think Nina's right. Anyway, it doesn't matter. We'll all be gone soon.'

'Not for a year and a half. I wonder where we'll all be then?' said Rose. 'Patti'll be at Oxford.'

'I'd rather be a Land Girl. Like farming camp really, only all the time.'

Nina shuddered. 'Oh Patti! That ghastly uniform! And all females! D'you think they'll really call us up?'

'How lovely,' said Rose. 'I'd be a nurse.'

'You'd have to go where they sent you. Anyway, it might not be till we're twenty.'

'I'd like to be a nurse.'

. . .

Dreams. Twenty miles from the spires of Moscow Hitler has stopped, snowblind, and now comes the counter-offensive. Olga the Boots has brought up a cabbage soup and Miss Winterton has confined all junior classes to their form rooms at recreation time for the duration of her fancy. And Sophy in her dream of chloral or laudanum hears voices, hears Moscow and rides a sleigh like the Snow Queen, singing in French through clouds of snow, spilling her burning jewels to warm the cold hands of young men; ice cracking, a bestiary of helmets, some other, dream war. Then in the white desert lies a boy with stubbled grey hair and no face. Heini!

Laura dreamed of a train, an endless train through a dark country and at no station had she the right to get off for she had no country. Always cold, more climbed on the train and more at each station and none she knew; faces pressed to the window, she searched them all, gaunt death's heads, women with starved babies; then a girl she had played with in Paris, an old madwoman who danced in a red skirt in the gardens of Berlin and once Maman in the green dress passed smiling through the carriage. Scotty discussed Proust with Mam'selle and Miss Winterton carried a whip. Heini, she mumbled, Papa, Patti? Laura half-woke and found the eiderdown had slipped off and thought of Stephen who said he dreamed of her every night. But his face too, slipped away and away until it was small as Scotty's, waving goodbye at the Gare St. Lazare, Scotty gone into the same darkness as Heini. As Maman, whose darkness was in her head.

It was musty in the shelter and Laura hated to go underground but with so few raids now, Stephen said, it was safe. Laura shuddered. A spider. They went mostly at night, now Olga was back, and sometimes at dinner-break. They lay under the rough grey blanket which scratched her bare skin only his flesh could warm. Was this love? Sometimes she laughed. It made the dreams better. It did heal.

While Patti wrote:

I don't want to go to Oxford or do Latin. I keep dreaming of that little girl on the spikes. I think sometimes that in the camp, or the school or the desert or the country, or just in our heads, we are all behind bars. That's silly, I know, and it's probably because I'm hating school or missing Laura. I try to think that you will come home and I remember how lovely it was on the farm. A lot of people say it's good about the Japanese bombing Pearl Harbour because now the Americans will come in. But the war's too big, I can't really see it. Does that sound awful when I'm supposed to be nearly grown up? I'm even old enough to be in love, like Laura. And all I can see is people looking at other people through bars. There's a boy in the Arboretum camp and I think about him. I mean prisoners.

The Yanks were coming. What would that mean? 'Late as usual,' murmured Lucy Trott and there were those who agreed. There was a new Art mistress, Miss Drinkwater, who wore billowing smocks and bare feet in thonged sandals in December. She bounded around the school like a large, friendly dog, taking big, bouncing strides, looking for a soul-mate. She said to the class: 'I hope we'll be pals.'

It was a tiring winter. The school was nervy. There was an outbreak of chicken-pox. Tempers and passions flared. There was petty thieving from lockers and no one showed much enthusiasm for the Christmas Bazaar for Funds for the Troops. The idea was you brought in something you didn't want and bought something else someone else didn't want and that was supposed to make money.

Laura was away. Lower Sixth T sat in the art room at the top of Albert Lodge (the studio roof of glass boarded over for the duration), waiting for Miss Drinkwater who believed in Free Expression. Posy scratched her chilblains. Patience was making her mind a blank, an absolute empty blank. It was blue. There was the general buzz of bored waiting and above it a voice, quite clear.

'Where's Lady Laura?' A giggle. Then someone said in a loud voice: 'Laura Meister's mother's potty.'

'She isn't.'

'And her father's a spy. He's in a camp. So there!'

Patience held on to her blue and silent vacancy. There was such quietness and stillness; the rain ran down the windows, tear after silent tear. Patience clenched her fists under the desk then the silence was broken like glass, shattered, as Rose of all people leapt like a tigress at Baxter and her gang, indiscriminately pulling plaits, scratching, sobbing, shouting: 'She's not! She's not!' Desks were thumped, yells like a football game or a murder or a killing, Rose's cheek was bleeding but she too had drawn blood.

There was a hush, like a whisper passed down the class from the door where Miss Drinkwater stood, appalled, her hands to her face.

'Perhaps someone will tell me what this disgraceful scene is all about? Someone? Patience? Nina?'

Patience looked at a small blue flower someone had put in a jam jar on the art table where she sat, and wondered where they could have found that, in winter? She said nothing. She held her silence. She would not spill one drop.

Repercussions.

Laura had had asthma but she was better now. She was afraid it might be the secret trysts in the shelter and, of course, she could admit that to no one. It had been awful, propped up in bed with that horrid inhaler, catching her breath, knowing Stephen would be waiting and there was no way of sending him a message. If Patience would come. Olga the Boots fussed in and out, pleased to have two patients, and Laura wished she would go away. Scotty had been the only one who ever helped: 'Hold my shoulders. Breathe like this.' And Papa sometimes, but he loved me too much.

The first break-time, she caught Patience before she could slip off to the library.

'What's this Nina told me? About a fight?'

Patience clearly didn't want to answer. Laura thought she looked tired. She was carrying a pile of books and paused, reluctantly, at the library door.

'Oh, just some silly row. Nothing really.'

'That's not what Nina said.'

'Then you'd better ask Nina.'

'Patti, why are you avoiding me?'

'Sorry. I didn't know I was.' There was Miss Trott, coming towards them down the corridor. 'I've got to go now, Laura.'

In the end it was Rose in the boiler-room who admitted: 'They were saying stupid things about your mother and father. I didn't help at all, I just made it worse. It must be the Irish, I suppose. It comes out sometimes.'

'She was brave,' said Posy. 'An absolute heroine! If you'd seen her, Laura, going for Baxter and the whole lot!' Then she drooped a little. 'There's going to be the most frightful row.'

Rose stood before Miss Trott and Miss Winterton.

'Simply tell the truth,' said Miss Trott. 'That is all we ask, Rose.'

'Someone said Laura Meister's mother was mad and her father was a spy in a prison camp.' Rose had never been in the Head's study before. She felt she wanted to pee, terribly.

'And who started this shameful scene?'

'I did, Miss Trott.'

'Address yourself to Miss Winterton.' Miss Winterton sat behind her desk. She had a hair growing out of a mole on her chin. She wore spectacles on a ribbon round her neck. She looked cold and grey, like a straight tree in winter without leaves. Miss Trott continued. 'And can you tell me why you took it upon yourself to attack another girl, physically, to behave like a barbarian?'

'I was angry.'

'Speak up, Rose, please. And where would we be, do you suppose, if everyone who was angry attacked someone else?'

'I don't know, Miss Trott.'

'We would have anarchy, Rose. You understand me? Rule by a chaotic mob. You will look up anarchy in the dictionary and write Miss Winterton a six-page essay on anarchy through history. You may go now, Rose. That will be all for the moment.'

Rose, having expected to be hanged by the neck until she was dead, was puzzled. She sat in the loo for a long time, thinking, and decided they were simply spinning out the execution. There would be worse to come.

'Such a quiet girl,' said Miss Winterton. 'I'm surprised.'

'Irish.'

'Ah, yes.'

'Not such a bad plan, to transfer the Dutch to Ireland and vice-versa. The Dutch would make a garden of Ireland, you see, and the Irish would drown.'

'Hitler?'

'Bismarck.'

Miss Trott and Miss Drinkwater saw Miss Winterton.

Miss Mallard saw Miss Trott. Terms were agreed. Perhaps a secret treaty.

Miss Drinkwater was out of her depth, as though she had stepped, unarmed and without warning, into a world war.

Barbara Baxter saw Miss Winterton and came out smirking.

Mam'selle tried to intervene but no one heard her.

Miss Lowrie felt sorry for little Rose Delane, but what could one do?

'You were so right, Claire, as always. The German girl must go.'

Claire smiled. 'I was thinking of Derbyshire for Christmas?'

Yes, Lucy would like that very much. It was nice to be comfortable with Claire again, in the winter study, with the curtains drawn. 'Of course, one could not actually sack her?'

'Not exactly.'

Lucy stirred the tiny fire. She shivered, had an odd premonition of something lost and irrecoverable, sacrificed. She would take mittens to Derbyshire, her bones were cold. Lucy pulled herself together. She poked the fire again, with vigour, and the sparks flew up.

Miss Winterton spoke. There was no doubt about her splendour, austere though it was. She spoke of Standards. She spoke of Rules.

She spoke of Purity, Leadership, Example, the Good of the Whole. Her deep voice could be thrilling and the occasion was with her. Everyone knew now about the fight in the art room and rumour fed speculation. Laura Meister's father was really Rudolf Hess. Laura was a Jew. Her mother had bitten out her own tongue with madness even in a strait-jacket. The little girls were seized by a fervour they did not understand, and with that same fervour they would have died for Miss Winterton. Instead, they sang 'Jerusalem', and as they swore never to cease a fight they barely grasped, their voices rose in the Christmas-decorated Hall, a few dancing like angels at the top of war's meagre Christmas tree.

Laura and her mother took rooms just for Christmas, to be near the doktor. It had been difficult to shake off Olga the Boots, who, having established herself as Sophy's nurse, protector and confessor, followed them to the station, thrusting upon them all the way and at the last moment, untidy, crumpled little parcels containing heaven-knew-what. Even as the train drew out, there she still was – an eccentric, stumpy little figure, in black lumpy skirt, man's water-proof cloak and the everlasting kerchief knotted behind her head; panting to keep up with the train, still calling after them in a rag-bag of languages advice, blessings, reproaches perhaps? Who could tell? Laura, leaning from the carriage window waved and waved. The least she could do. And was reminded of Scotty and that other parting, in Paris. Her eyes stung, though she did not cry, and her tears would not have been for Olga.

Their quarters were two rooms in a pretty enough cottage not far from the gates of the house. Their landlady – her husband away in the army – was a decent woman with little to say, but correct. They met mostly at meal-times when Papa was not free. Sometimes he had to work at strange hours, even in the night. At first, Laura took up her mother's breakfast to bed, but after two days of country air and seeing Papa, Maman came down to breakfast with Laura, Mrs Moffat and her daughter – a girl of about eleven, with round pudding face and a relentless stare. After some desultory talk among her elders about weather and rationing, the silent Audrey, spoon halfway to her mouth, suddenly spoke:

'Are you Nazis?'

'Mind your tongue, Audrey.' Mrs Moffat slapped her daughter's hand. 'Get down now and feed the chickens.'

'I don't want to.'

'You'll do what I say.'

When her daughter had left the room, unwillingly, dragging her feet and gazing back at her mother's peculiar guests, Mrs Moffat squeezed another cup of watery tea from the pot.

'It's that place over there, you see,' she said flatly. 'She spoke out of turn, but then we don't know what's going on. If it's a camp or if it's not a camp. The guards, you see, then all those foreigners walking about, coming into the village.'

'I'm sorry, Mrs Moffat,' said Laura, 'but then we don't really know either. Even my father can't tell us much – or he's not allowed to. But he's not a Nazi, truly, any more than we are. In fact, that's partly why he's there.'

Mrs Moffat looked into her teapot as if it might tell her the future or the truth. Then she sighed and put on the lid.

'It's a funny old war.'

They were allowed in some kind of lounge or recreation room: much more comfortable than the one at the first camp.

'You see,' said Papa, 'Just like the drawing-room of an English country house – and that is exactly what it is.' Deep, comfortable chairs and sofas, covered in a spludgy flower pattern, low tables, lamps, magazines, even an elderly labrador with a grey muzzle who seemed to have formed a particular attachment to the doktor. So on Christmas Day, while Sophy rested, Laura and her father, followed by the dog, took a walk. There was no snow, but a nip in the air, and Papa put his arm round Laura's shoulder.

'You are warm enough, little Lolly? You look tired, but different? I think you are happier?'

'Yes, Papa, I am much happier.'

'You have a beau?'

'There's a boy I like. Yes. But please don't tell Maman – there's nothing bad about him, but there's a reason truly, I don't want her to see him.'

Her father nodded. He called up Blackie the labrador and Laura thought of Rover, the English dog she and Heini had invented in the Berlin gardens. That was a recollection she must block off, like so many, like closing a door.

They had reached the top of the hill and looked over to the South Downs. Up here there had been the merest frosting of snow, the ruts of the plough were frozen and below them lay a field, it seemed, of flints. What a strange landscape, Laura thought, whatever could you grow here but a harvest of stones. The sky was wide and white, it seemed an old place, inviolable – yet below beyond the barbed-wire fence, was a crater. What would there be to bomb here?

'Jerry,' said her father, 'ditches them on the way home.' His tone was sardonic, pained. 'At least here they hurt no one.' He pointed with his stick to some odd but natural-seeming formations on the facing hill, crowned by a clump of trees. 'Iron Age fortifications. And up there, they say, a temple once, Iron Age, then Roman. The story is, you run round seven times at night with a bowl of porridge and the devil comes out of the trees. History, myth, nonsense, it consoles a little.'

'Could we see it?'

Papa tapped the fence with his stick. 'Here I may go and no further – without a pass. This is my boundary.' He turned to go down, taking Laura's elbow. 'You know, it reminds me of boarding-school.'

'But now you've taken their offer, you're doing their work?'

'Then now, it is a very comfortable boarding-school.'

Laura knew better than to ask more. They went down.

At the gate he paused. The dog looked up for orders and Papa said: 'Your mother, she is not well, I know that. You find it difficult but I must ask you, Lolly, to be patient. And not to be ashamed if sometimes you cannot be patient. She is one of those who do not find it easy to live in the world and it is worse now for her.'

Yet at the Christmas lunch, to which they were admitted, Sophy dazzled, as she could. Charmed and teased and they all drank a little too much, even Laura. The clever men Papa worked with wore paper

131

hats and courted her and Laura could see that her mother was brilliant, she had this gift of shrugging off her darkness like a dusty cloak and even these dry men in this strange prison, even Laura, were enchanted, caught in her loom.

They sang carols and played silly games, then in the late afternoon, Papa saw them to the cottage. It was a clear night. He kissed them both and said gently, solemnly. 'My dear loves. You see we may still be together. Christ is born again.'

Mrs Moffat was sitting by the wireless, her hands unusually empty, Audrey nowhere to be seen. She stirred herself and made cocoa they did not want, but drank politely, the mood of the party still on them. Then she said, putting down the mug, and sitting, her hands flat on the table: 'They've just said. Hong Kong's gone. That's where he was.' Sophy murmured something, Laura too tried to speak, to touch, to help, but the woman just sat and watched them drink. Then she looked up straight in their faces, first one, then the other, and said: 'Get out of my house.'

Rose's trial had been conducted in camera and without evidence of witness, even of the villainess herself.

The first day of the new term, poor Rose was sick in prayers. Every day of the Christmas holidays, she had visited the Cathedral and lit a candle to a different saint, just to cover all eventualities; though she liked the Virgin best, she had a kind face and such a nice baby. It seemed odd to no one that she had been obliged to await her fate right through the holiday, praying and being sick and not eating, until the boiler-room crowd considered her with real anxiety. Patience and Laura had helped her with her essay for Miss Winterton but there was nothing else anyone could do but await Recrimination.

'Rose,' said Laura, 'I'm sorry. And it was all because of me.'

'It was all because of Barbara Baxter,' said Nina firmly. She offered Rose a cigarette.

'No thank you,' said Rose, 'I think I'd be sick.'

And then, after all that, she was let off as misguided (presumably by Laura Meister) and spring came and with spring the Yanks, cowboys strutting long-legged around the town as if they owned it.

Rumour, however, once kindled, did not die but ran beneath the earth. There were eyes, there were stories, there were whispers, all for Laura.

Patience lay awake. On and on they went, a ceaseless drone. She heard her mother stir, move around her room, and still they came.

Laura lay with Stephen in the school shelter, though this was getting dangerous, these lighter evenings.

'It must be a hundred,' she whispered.

'More like a thousand.'

They crept to the mouth of the shelter and peered out: an incredible sight, like whales in the sky, an endless, heavy moving shoal.

Laura said: 'I think I'd like to go home.'

'It's all right. They're ours.' Stephen realised what he had said.

'Oh, love, I'm sorry.' She made him feel like a plough-boy sometimes. That he should have captured her at all astounded him: always he felt she might slip through his fingers. 'I'm an idiot.'

'No. Really, it doesn't matter. I mean, I'm not really German, I'm not anything.' She sank back against the sandbags at the entrance. 'Fighting though. I just wish they'd stop.'

'I suppose I'll have to join up soon. Well, everyone is – at the end of term, in the summer. Even those who don't have to.'

She nodded, having half-expected this. But it was still a shock. She clung to him as though physically to hold him from leaving.

And the bombers went on and on.

'It is the invasion!' cried Olga the Boots and, fortunately for Laura, creeping in near dawn, put her pillow over her head, and a saucepan on top.

'Mais Cologne!' cried Mam'selle next morning in the staffroom. '*Elle est si belle*! The Cathedral!'

'Piffle,' said Josephine Mallard. 'Serve them right for Coventry. That reminds me, number two shelter is unsafe. Better close it pro tem.'

Violetta Lowrie looked sympathetically at Mam'selle, and sighed. Sanity was the first casualty of war, beauty the next. Without looking up from her book, she could sense Drinkwater bearing down on her, wanting to be a pal, and talk about art. It was like having a horse on your lap. Miss Lowrie closed her book, smiled vaguely and slipped out of the room.

Nina had a Yank who gave her nylon stockings, better even than silk. It was a dancing summer for her, at the Palais or the American Club where everyone thought she was twenty and she sat on a high bar stool and drank whisky and kissed. She loved the way they talked and smelled and kissed: it was as simple as that. Nina got away with it. Nina could get away with anything. She simply didn't care if she were caught and expelled – though she'd miss the gang, she said. 'You know, men are all right, but you can't really talk to them.'

Hardly a bomb dropped from the sky that summer, where they were; they were at the still centre of a holocaust and sometimes could see the fires burning in the distance.

Patti wrote:

Everyone tells you this is the happiest time of your life, because you're young, but it seems to me very difficult being young, I mean being the age I am. Perhaps it's the war, but I don't think so. I feel different things almost every day, even about my friends at school. That foreign girl I told you about, Laura, wants to make friends again, I know, and so do I. Then the next day I nearly hate her. She's like that – the sort of person you can only love or only hate, and it's not her fault. If it's anyone's fault it's ours or the teachers' or the school's. The thing is, she doesn't fit in, she's not like anyone else.

I wonder if the world is like the school? I don't mean home, that's different, but the whole world? Is it like that in the army, where you are?

Rotten exams soon. Working quite hard because I know that people (that is mother and Miss Trott) want me to go to university, though (this is a secret) I'd rather be in the country. That was lovely, last summer, at the camp. It seemed so silly that you were fighting the Italians and the Italians we met were so sweet and funny, they didn't want to fight anyone. We used to sing in French. Rommel is different I expect.

There's hardly any bombing here now. You might not believe there's a war on, except for the Americans and shopping. And yet I have this feeling that something awful is going to happen. It might not be the war – in fact, I'm sure it's something else.

We haven't heard from you for two months but mother says that's to be expected. You seem so far away. Please be careful. Everyone says Rommel is very clever.

'Patti, please, let's be friends again?'

The two girls were in the summer bivouac, among the rhododendrons.

'Was it Stephen?' Laura continued.

'I don't know. A bit.'

'Because he's joined up, you know. He needn't have done. I did love him. But people don't stay. They're always going away. Will you come home for tea? We could do our prep together. It'll be like old times!' Laura seized her hands. She was too bright, glass that might crack. In a lower voice she said, 'You know why it was Stephen, don't you?'

'Heini?'

'Oh, Patti, you do understand! You're the only one who does.'

Just for a moment, in the shade, Laura looked like the oldest woman of time, a girl with hollowed face and eyes, beneath the dusty leaves. 'I looked in the Bible,' she said, in a voice so faint Patience could hardly catch it. 'I think that was a sin, to love my brother so much. But I can't believe that, can you – that any love can be wicked?'

At the same moment, the two girls moved together. It was hardly even a kiss.

They walked back past the camp where, in the wavering summer light and heat, the men, stripped to the waist, were doing physical jerks. Click Clack!

The girls walked, heads bent towards each other, out of the light into the dimness of the school.

12

It was as though everything continued as it had been, but beneath some great sea-change were toiling, that would alter everything. Perhaps the 'something awful' Patience had anticipated. Perhaps it was simply growing up. Or being the age they were.

'To be young,' said Mam'selle, pouring watery tea in her dark little room that smelled of cat and dust and something sweeter, like pot-pourri. She looked at Laura and Patience, her eyes sharp and sad. Laura and Patience: the two girls came together now, Laura had brought her friend. Laura asked first long ago because one was sorry for her, because both were *dépaysée* and then one enjoyed speaking French for pleasure, without teaching. And now the little Meister girl brought Patience, Anglo-Saxon – so large these young women on this draughty island: giantesses who lived with windows flung open; but a nice child. Mam'selle lost, then caught the cobweb of her thought: 'To be young in the middle of a war is to be a child who hears her parents. They are quarrelling in another room. She may know that one is right, the other hurt. But she is still bewildered. There will be the same pain.'

This was only Patience's second visit. She was still shy but she found herself liking the French teacher, gaining courage in her company.

'Most of us don't think very much about the war, Mam'selle. I mean, unless it hurts us, ourselves. There's school and home, you see. I suppose that's rather awful. It must be much worse for you and Laura.'

'That is quite right, Patience, that you should think about home and school.'

Laura was clearly at home here. She sat on the floor by Mam'selle's chair. She said very little. Patience had the impression that this was a place she rested, like a bird on a branch. When they had finished tea, Mam'selle knitted in that funny French way that appeared so fast and difficult: with the cat on her lap, it looked as though she were knitting a cat, for wool and animal were both of the same fluffy, dowdy texture. The cat's eyes were gummy and it had a bare patch halfway down its spine.

Mam'selle sighed and smiled. '*Ma pauvre Minette.*'

Laura stirred dreamily. 'Would you tell Patience about Paris, Mam'selle? Please?'

'About Paris? Well! When I was young, there was the convent, and we all wore sailor suits and hats and walked in crocodiles. You would never believe how strict. Then the Lycée – hard work but some wickedness too. The same the world over, you see. There was a young man, a cousin, picnics at Fontainebleau, but always with the family. He tried to grow a little moustache and there was a boat. We slipped away. So hot.' The needles had ceased to fly in the teacher's arthritic claws, and for a moment she might have dozed, but then said quite clearly: 'I was young. I was often cross. That is normal. One day my father – he was an *avocat* but adored the literature – he took me for a walk in the park and pointed to a man: that is Monsieur Proust, he said. I thought he was ugly and I didn't care. But you were asking about Paris?'

Laura stood. 'Thank you very much for tea, Mam'selle. I think we should go now.'

The little woman nodded. 'You know your way out. Come again, my dears.' Just as they reached the door, she called after them: 'Next time I shall tell you about Paris!'

'I thought she was going to drop off,' said Patience, 'like the dormouse in *Alice*. She's nice. Why does she wear a wig? Was she in love with that boy in the boat? Why didn't she marry him?'

'He was killed, you know, in that other war. So her hair fell out.'

'You're making that up! Cousins can't marry anyhow, or if they do they have peculiar babies.'

Laura grinned. 'Ask her yourself! Come on – come back with me and we'll do our prep together.'

'She must be terribly old.'

'Who?'

'To have been in that other war.'

In Laura's tower room, Patience said to the ceiling: 'Fancy being in love like that.'

'Like what?' Laura sat on the edge of the bed and poked her finger in Patience's ribs.

'Ouch! So that your hair falls out. It's rather romantic. Did you love Stephen like that?'

'Never mind. If you don't shut up I'll tickle you to death.'

'I'm not ticklish.'

'Yes, you are! I can feel.'

'It's too hot. Stop it!'

'Keep still or you'll burst the springs.'

'I'm stronger than you!'

Laughter, heat, and now Patience had turned, had Laura pinned to the bed by her arms.

'Pax!'

There was just one moment, a flicker, a question, an urge that made Patience shiver, wonder as the reflection of the water-green midsummer leaves crashed against the roof of the little attic. Silence. Broken. Laura's echo.

'Pax.'

The dangerous shelter was closed, pro tem, as Mallard said, but it was used: another of the secret bivouacs for Miss Trott to keep her eye on. Useful, for since the official tightening-up the Arboretum had been forbidden even to the sixth form within school hours. It was Posy who, with astonishing resourcefulness, had found the way in at the back – under a tree, behind a bush, a corrugated iron sheet that could be easily pulled aside.

'Like a burrow,' she said, then squeaked at a brooding spider.

Rose at once converted it to a home. The floor was swept, even a few old cushions brought for the hard bench seats, so you could lie down. The green light from the outside was enough, filtered by the leaves. When they had smoked or eaten there, Rose, Mrs Tittlemouse, tidied up the stubs and scraps and took them all away.

It was also forbidden even to walk with a High School boy in Albert Road.

'What do they think we are?' groaned Nina. 'Virgins?'

'Well, I am,' said Rose crossly, while Posy blushed for what she did not understand.

Nina turned over on her stomach and flicked cigarette ash on the floor.

'Well, we're old enough to be married. And have babies, God forbid. More than those old cows have ever done.'

Patience wondered. 'Mallard's not that old. But I can't imagine her having babies.'

Nina lowered her voice, for Posy not to hear.

'Don't you know about Mallard? She's moved in with Drinkwater.'

'Well, why not?'

'If you don't know what I mean,' Nina replied airily, 'I'm not telling. Not for me to pollute your pure young ears.'

Patience didn't like Nina so much since she started going out with those Americans. Why had she changed so, she wondered? Was it love? Laura had been in love, but she hadn't changed. What happened to people? It seemed sad when you thought about it – her own mother loved her father, so she must be very lonely, though she never said so. And poor Mrs Meister, she must once have been so beautiful. And Nina, doing whatever she did with those Americans who gave her real nylon stockings: she'd roll her eyes and say she was crazy about so-and-so, but if that was love, it hadn't made her nicer, and you'd expect it to, surely? Patience studied Nina, sprawled on the bench reading some silly magazine Miss Trott would certainly confiscate if she found it, and thought perhaps it's just that she's terribly sexy. And if you're like that, you can't help it, your body has to do it, like being hungry and having to eat. That would be called lust. And those big, fair men with funny accents who grinned and whistled and looked like film stars – a lot of people didn't like them, said they'd taken over the country and got girls into trouble; but

Patience tried to imagine why Nina would fancy them, not just for the presents they gave her.

Now Patience was pretending to read but she was remembering when they were young and swopped dirty bits from the Bible about a man 'knowing' a woman: there was a lot about knowing in the Old Testament. Now, of course, she understood what it meant, more or less, and suddenly was ashamed because she terribly wanted to discover if Nina 'knew' her Yanks. And if it was wrong, and if she herself would like it. She thought not.

Suddenly she wondered if Laura had known Stephen?

'What's up, Patti? Goose crossed your grave?'

Patience shook her head and buried her face in *The Faerie Queene*.

'Well,' sighed Rose, 'if Miss Lowrie had babies they'd be absolutely beautiful.'

Nina threw a cushion at her.

The bell rang and they left the shelter, with intervals between, approaching the school building from different directions, casually; the last one out put back the corrugated iron and pulled the bush across it. That was how you tricked the guards in films. Patience was the first out. Laura had been reading through all this, and, just for the moment, Patience didn't terribly want to talk to her.

The camp trembled in the midday sun, might have dissolved. There had been a change lately. In the mornings, when the girls arrived at school, they would see two lorry-loads of prisoners being taken out and driven away. Nina said they were probably going to shoot them, to frighten Posy, but someone else knew they were working somewhere, as farm-hands, like the Italians. It wasn't like the Italians, though: there were two guards to each lorry and no one was singing. Those left behind seemed dispirited, ghostly in the shaking light thrown up from the earth in which they scratched, tending the plots half-heartedly. The boy with the shaved head they had noticed in the winter must have been ill, because sometimes he would stand for hours with his hands clutching at the inner wire, still wearing his greatcoat, even on the hottest day; then he might walk the whole perimeter, still touching the wire every few yards, as though looking for a door. The girls who had to cross the Arboretum

140

to reach the school took a longer way round not to see him, or quickened their pace. They could not call him loopy any more, nor could they speak of him, or understand why they ran from him, when he could do them no harm.

Swotting. Exams. French orals.

'*Où est-ce-que vous allez pendant les vacances, Patience?*'

'*Je vais à la campagne, Mademoiselle.*'

At least, I hope so, thought Patience. Farming camp would be nice if Laura could come. Or mother even says we could go to the Manifold Valley again and take Laura (but I don't know if she means Mrs Meister too). These orals aren't too bad, after all, perhaps because Mam'selle is nice and you know she wants you to get it right. It's raining. I do hope it's not going to be a rotten summer. Mam'selle's broken her spectacles and stuck them together with Elastoplast. Laura's next after me – she'll sail through, of course.

Should it have been '*je vais aller*'?

I said Laura hadn't changed but she has a bit. Not harder – she could never be that – but quieter when we're with other people, and as if she might suddenly say something quite sharp. Stronger? Do I mean stronger? Perhaps preparing herself – arming. Yes, that's the word: arming.

Only twenty minutes to go and I never know what to say about Luther. Trotty seems to approve of him but he always seems so glum to me, though of course he was brave. I read somewhere that he had awful constipation, but I can't put that in, though it would explain a lot. If it hadn't been for him we might all be Catholics still like Rose. That must be easier because you have Faith and if you break the rules you have to say and get a sort of punishment. Their churches smell nicer, too, but I'm not sure – it must be rather like being a child or a prisoner.

When we're alone, Laura isn't much different really. But with other people she seems to be there and not there somehow. Older. She has to be, I expect, because of looking after her mother. She's cut her hair so that it only just touches her collar and has a fringe in front now. She's reading Colette – Mam'selle says she's a frightfully good writer but you have to read her in French or you miss something.

English. Well, that's easy. Though I've gone off Wordsworth and all those silly daffodils. He never seems to look *at* Nature, just at himself looking at Nature; as if you were supposed to clap.

I wonder why all the poets we do have to be dead?

Laura looked at her mother, pushing Olga's junket round the bowl. She tried to feel. She neither loved her nor hated her. She felt nothing. That was terrible. I shall talk to the doctor, she thought, and then I shall go to the camp.

'*Manges*, Maman,' she said, very gently. 'Just a little more? One spoon?'

'That Hungarian idiot is poisoning me.' Pettishly, Sophy Meister pushed aside Laura's spoon.

'It's good for you. Please Maman.'

'Babies' food. For the nursery. For babies. You know, you were an ugly baby, Lolly. A little yellow shrivelled head after all those hours of labour. Heini was easy. I've told you, how easily he came? The next week I was dancing! Did I tell you? Heini's not dead?'

'We don't know, Maman.'

Laura felt nothing for her mother and yet she could have wept. Was that love? Her mother caught her sleeve, pulled her down towards the pillow. There were days when Laura could have cradled her mother and wept with her, keening together in whatever mad country Sophy visited with her tears. 'We must be careful,' her mother hissed, 'of that woman in the kitchen. That kitchen-maid. If she were not such a wretched creature, I would send her away.'

'Maman, Olga isn't our servant,' said Laura clearly, explaining to a child. 'She helps us. She is good. We can't send her away. Now I'll give you your medicine and sit with you. Then you must go to sleep.'

It had started soon after the Christmas visit to Papa. Maman was always more disturbed than usual when she'd seen him and poor Mrs Moffat had made it much worse. All the way home she had been very quiet, and for a week afterwards. Almost meekly, she had tried to help Olga in the kitchen, appeared to attend to Olga's endless, multilingual gossip which massacred at least three languages in the telling.

Then one day Laura got home from school to find Olga alone, banging saucepans around. Maman, she indicated with shrugs and thumps, had locked herself in her room and would not come out. Oh no! She had not suicided herself for one could hear her talking and moving around, *nein? n'est-ce-pas?*

Indeed, one could, until the door was finally flung open and there was Sophy wearing her very best Worth and the hat she used to call her flirting hat, with the tiny sparkling eye-veil, make-up thick white and lips purple, entertaining, among the little chairs and rugs and shawls and bibelots, a roomful of invisible guests.

Another time, evading the watchful Olga – without whose help Laura could not have gone to school – she put on some dirty old smock she had found in the dusting-rag cupboard, and shaved her head so close to the scalp she had, in places, drawn a little blood. They were watched, she said. They must sit very still.

Laura knelt on the floor and took her mother's hands.

'Maman, Olga is not watching you, she is looking after you. She is our friend.'

'You see, Laura,' Sophy said in a voice that was almost reasonable, though whispered: 'I am a prisoner. They have sent your father away and put us in a prison.'

'That was ages ago, Maman, and only a few. It never happened to us – you and me. They have been very good to us in England.'

'Poor Lolly. You are too young for prison.'

The tired doctor was not very interested in the paranoid delusions of hysterical refugees, though he was sorry for the girl. Meister? That was a German name, wasn't it? Jews, he supposed.

'No. My father was what you would call a liberal. He said things in the university that Hitler did not like. My brother betrayed him and now he's missing. My brother, I mean. My mother loved him very much, and she loves my father too. So you can see.'

Laura stood with the heavy man in the kitchen. Her father came for a day. Sophy refused absolutely to return to that village, to find another lodging, to be near him. When he left she was surprisingly controlled. The doctor prescribed. Sophy improved a little. The doctor was not hard. War rode him like a hag. The girl looked peaky. Yes, she should get off for a bit. He'd pop in and there was the old girl from downstairs. Though reluctant to commit the Meister woman, privately it was beyond him. He moved awkwardly, too big, soft bellied, in the small, cluttered room.

'What are you reading, Lolly?'

She was not asleep, after all, though she must have dozed. Her face looked fresher.

'Colette, Maman.'

'Which?'

'*La Vagabonde.*'

'Ah, yes! We are both *vagabondes* you and I. I feel better. Read to me, Lolly.'

Mary Mackenzie, resting in a deck-chair, looked up to find Patience blocking the sun. Patience had still not fined down – now she probably never would; it was awkward without Graham, and Patience at this age. No longer a child. She needed her father, they both did, through whom to readjust their relationship. They were shy with each other: as two women might be, one young, one older, who find themselves in the same railway carriage, obliged to converse.

Mary would have liked to talk of Graham. Perhaps Patience would. But they were English, their mouths were stuffed with reticence, with the space the English allow one another, at least in Spring Gardens.

'Yes, of course you must go to the camp. You enjoyed it last year.'

Patience shifted. 'But will you be all right? Alone, I mean, at the farm?'

Mary smiled, that little curve of the lips with which she so often surveyed the world: 'I don't imagine I shall be attacked by bandits.' She picked up the magazine she had closed when Patience appeared in the garden. There was the sweet smell of mown grass. As some of the first-comers to Spring Gardens, their hedges were well established, thick and high as walls. It was pretty: Mary had an eye for a garden as well as a painting. You have an eye for a garden, Graham always said, and once, before Patience was born, he had teased her, one warm night scented with nicotiana and stock, to make love in the small orchard. She saw over his shoulder the moon through the trees, full. If you see the full moon in the desert, he said, you go blind, sometimes mad – though how would he know that then? Did he sleep now, did he close his eyes? There was Patience, still there. 'Did you know,' said her mother, 'it says here that unless it was in the national interest, everyone with a book due to be published had it returned at the outbreak of war? How terrible that must have been. Laura's going, is she, to the camp? Then you'll have a lovely time.'

Mary and her daughter would kiss once during the day: good night. They would lie awake sometimes, each listening for the other to call. Listening to their silence.

They would have a lovely time, and if it was not quite the same, well, how could that be expected?

No Boys' High, in the first place. Old Winterboots had fixed that, Nina said. There were rumours of a small caucus growing to unseat Miss Winterton! Unheard-of heresy, but there were those, up there, who felt that there had become something manic about the Head's autocracy. 'Rules!' snapped Lowrie one day, uncharacteristically cross, 'this school is becoming like a prison camp.' Mam'selle wagged agreement and even Mallard's pal, Drinkwater, had quite an upsetting little scrap with Josephine on the subject. 'Honestly, Jo, they're not criminals – they're girls!'

It didn't matter much anyway, because most of the boys they'd known had gone: Jack to the army, Stephen to the RAF.

So though it was the same house, it was a different farm and, a few fields away, Germans instead of those lovely Italians. They worked harder, the farmer said, and if you asked him, he'd swop you two macaroni merchants for one Nazi. The girls did not meet the Germans, who travelled in their own lorries, under guard. They saw them only in the distance, figures shaking in the light across the flat fields, except once when they went to cool their feet in the old pond.

Patience first said 'Stop' and signalled to the others, be quiet, be still. Nina crept up behind her.

'What is it? Who's there?'

'Ssh. Men. I think they're Germans. They haven't seen us. Keep down.'

Sounds of churning water and shouts. The other girls had come up now and all crouched behind the leaves. Then Nina gasped.

'I say! Do look – they're starkers!'

'Shut up.'

'Look at that young one!' Nina hissed. 'Isn't he sweet? If only Laura were here, she'd know what they were saying. They are German, aren't they?'

'Must be.'

Rose blushed, but parted the leaves, just a little. 'We shouldn't watch.'

'Got to know sometime, Rosie,' said Nina. 'Aren't they funny with their little white bottoms, where the sun hasn't caught them. Like rabbit tails.'

Patience thought of Laura and Stephen there, last summer, dabbling their feet, their faces striped, as were the prisoners' bodies, with green and gold.

'We'd better go.'

Posy grinned. 'If they catch us, they'll rape us!'

'Don't be an idiot.'

Then Posy went quiet. They all did. They wanted to run yet all were held as though the sight of the thrashing, playing men had turned the girls to trees, transfixed them. Not merely the male anatomy, which was of course, interesting, though a little disappointing, but something about the light, and the porpoise-leaping frenzy of the bathers in the middle of the quiet wood. Then the Tommy, who had been sitting on the bank, smoking, fully dressed, stood, slung his rifle on his shoulder and called out: 'Come on you buggers, playtime's up.'

The girls crept on hands and knees for the first few yards, watching for twigs, till they could walk straight but silent still, clutching their sandals.

Only when they were out of the wood and standing again in the open at the edge of the field, did anyone speak.

'But that's *our* pond,' said Posy. 'They've spoiled it!'

Older now. Iron-framed beds in a fresh, white-painted room at the top of the house. Coarse white coverlets and even blue-white net curtains that billowed like veils in a day-time breeze. Older as they were, they had privileges they were pleased to receive. No snail races though. No Cordelia King either, with her airs.

'Isn't it funny – I never thought I'd miss *her*. I don't really, it's just that I was used to her, I suppose. She was always there.'

Potato picking made Laura cough in the night.

Night whispers.

'Laura? Laura, are you all right? Shall I get some water?'

'No. It's stopped. Thanks. I've got some water. But I'd love some air.'

'We can open the blackout. Look.'

Patience pulled back the curtain and opened the window between their beds. By moonlight, Laura looked ghostly, hardly there, the impression of a girl on a bed. She smiled. 'That's better.' Posy Potter gave a funny little snore. Rose mumbled and turned over. Baxter, thank heaven, slept in the other dorm, in charge of the little ones.

'I couldn't sleep either,' said Patience. 'It's so warm. Come on, kneel by the window, here. It's much better.'

The two girls knelt by the window. The lawn was moon-white, like snow. Laura still gasped.

'D'you want your inhaler?'

'No.' Laura took in a breath before she could speak. 'But if we could go outside.'

'Why not?'

'If we're caught?'

'It's only Lowrie and Mam'selle. They wouldn't mind. But there'll be dew. Take your cloak.'

The white lilies with their saffron eyes were over now and no flowers replaced them. Just the white grass and the tall boles of trees; the lawn was untended, cut but mossy, soft to tread barefoot. They trailed their own shadows like gowns behind them as they walked towards the seat at the edge of the ha-ha.

'D'you remember last summer?'

'Mm. I came a week late and you were dancing.'

Patience shook her head. 'No, I wasn't dancing. I was in the garden.' With Stephen, she thought.

147

Laura was breathing more easily now. She sat with her head tipped back, breathing deeply, so that her cloak fell away. Unlike the rest, she always wore not pyjamas but a nightdress of thin white cotton with a high neck and a pretty, hand-sewn yoke. ('But that's heaven!' Rose had breathed: 'the stitching!' Relic of Paris, when Maman had, in her vague way, supervised things like that. There was nothing she could supervise now.)

'How Maman would love it here. With servants, of course, and furniture. Wait till you see England, she always used to say. She had fun here once, poor Maman. Before she was married. With gentlemen attendants – quite innocent, of course. A lot of men were in love with her and she adored to dance.' An odd mood had caught Laura. She stood and, throwing off her cloak, did a twirl on the lawn. 'So do I. Scotty taught me. But I told you that. Come on, Patti, don't be a wallflower.'

'But you'll catch your death. And I'm hopeless. No music, anyway.'

'Come on! I'll show you! I'll hum.' That something about Laura lately that was silent, almost dull in company, then suddenly brittle and wild, bright as glass. But they did, they did dance and it was not so hard after all, till Patience tripped and they tumbled, laughing, tears of laughter streaming down their faces. They lay on the lawn, side by side, still holding hands.

'Oh, Patti, I feel so much better! As though it will all be all right now.'

They lay. Patience felt very calm and happy. They ought to move, she knew, the grass would be wet. She felt as one does in the sun, on a beautiful afternoon. Moonbathing.

'Did you know we saw some prisoners swimming in our pond this afternoon?'

'Rosie told me. Nude! she said, "not a holy thread".' Laura looked at the staring moon. 'Scotty always used to say that aesthetically – that's what she said – *aesthetically* the male form was, next to the female, inferior. I often wondered how she knew. From statues, I expect, if she could find one without a fig-leaf.'

'Laura? What was it like when Scotty kissed you?'

'Funny.' Laura pondered. 'Nice.'

Then they were both sitting up, kneeling face to face, solemnly and shyly. It was a dry and gentle kiss, so brief it might never have happened. Then Laura jumped to her feet, snatched up her cloak and they ran indoors across the moon-soaked lawn.

A day of rain that kept them indoors, mooning around, Mam'selle's arthritis played up and she cracked her knuckles between rows of knitting. The tension of boredom. Barbara had the little ones doing physical jerks till Miss Lowrie took pity on them and organised a treasure hunt all over the house, with clues and a whole bar of chocolate at the end.

Once they had made their beds, the little ones were not allowed back in their dormitories until evening, but this was another of the small sixth-form privileges. Chores done, they went upstairs to write letters, or play cards, or yawn. Nina smoked (definitely against the rules), but stopped amiably when Laura coughed.

Rose thought this must once have been the nursery. Her grandmother, she said, had been a nursery-maid in a place like this, so she knew.

'What a lot of babies,' marvelled Posy.

'Don't be silly. There'd only be four or five. But they used to put them upstairs with their own servants, away from the grown-ups.'

'Servants for babies!'

Only half-listening, Patience saw Nina, stretched on her bed, painting her toe-nails with American nail-varnish. Nina was always doing something to her body, her hair, her face. Now, apparently, she was satisfied, and lay on the bed in the grey light, reading a film magazine while her toe-nails dried. She had black hair and very white skin, and in her bra and pants, with just a thin cotton dressing-gown, she looked like one of those girls you see on calendars. Did Nina go out with her Americans because she wanted to be a film star? Once, when they were young, she'd told Patience that when she grew up she wanted to go to Hollywood. Lying there, her magazine slipped to the floor, her gaze on nothing, there was something dreaming about Nina, and waiting.

'Is it still raining?'

'Mmn.'

'It'll be muddy tomorrow. It gets in my ears.'

Only Posy could get mud in her ears. What she was doing in the Upper Sixth, no one knew: it was as though she had stayed on by accident, because no one noticed and told her to go.

The gang, thought Patience – we know each other better than we know our families, yet it will change, it will end, that will be sad.

Rose is the sweetest. Rose will change the least. I hope Rose never changes.

Laura. On the next bed, Laura asleep, or pretending to sleep, her face turned towards Patience but her eyes closed, shadowed by the dark fringe, the bedclothes rumpled – she seemed hardly there, the picture of a girl, like one of the Impressionists Mam'selle was upset about being buried; at one of their odd little teas, the French teacher had produced a book for Laura and Patience, of those vague girls in orchards, children paddling, dancers, sleepers. 'Caught always, you see, on the point of vanishing. That fragile moment. *Elles s'évanouient.*'

Nina had stirred and dragged out an old wind-up gramophone they had found in the cupboard. *We'll meet again, don't know where, don't know when.* Laura opened her eyes. She looked round puzzled, frowning.

'I was dreaming.'

'Are you worried about your mother?'

'Yes. I had a bad dream. Something about her. The doctor said I should come, and Olga. Papa – he wanted me to. Of course it's all right. I feel fuzzy. Come on, let's go for a walk. The rain's stopped.'

And so it had.

The rain-drops sparked. The earth steamed. A day or so later, it was dry again, thundery heat, friable soil, and it was exhausting work, mopping the sweat from your eyes as you picked and humped the potatoes to the weighing bag. The back of Patience's neck had caught the sun and she pulled up her collar. Boring Baxter in her Aertex shirt romped down the rows: she'd have the record weight for the day – she always did. Riding her bicycle peacefully along the tree-shaded lane, Violetta Lowrie paused and gazed across the flat fields: the landscape seemed immense, the horizon far away but very clear. There, in the distance, a small church squatted among low cottages; a dark tight-fisted cloud had gathered behind it in the white burned sky but the sun touched and fired a golden weather-cock on the steeple. Out in the open, between lane and village, the girls stooped and picked, stooped and picked. Millet? wondered Miss Lowrie, the Gleaners? She smiled, satisfied, and cycled on.

Posy running, crying even before she reached her: 'Patti! Come quickly! Laura's dying!'

Not dying at all, of course, but it was a bad attack and put Laura to bed. Nothing to worry about, young lady, just stay where you are. The times she'd heard that!

'Will you be all right?'

'Bless you, Patti, just bored. I could easily get up.'

'The doctor said you mustn't.'

'If only you could stay.'

'But I could! Today I could cycle back at lunch-time and after that I'll swop kitchen duties. That'll be easy!'

'Oh, Patti – whatever would I do without you?'

'Quite well, I expect.'

A sticky heat still, that sent Mam'selle and Miss Lowrie under the shade of the trees. They discussed Descartes and in the middle, Mam'selle dozed off; Miss Lowrie dreamed in her hammock.

The house was shaded, blind, still. In the white room, Patience sat on the edge of Laura's bed.

'What are you reading?'

'Colette. Lie down, you'll be more comfortable.'

'Read it to me?'

Laura grinned. 'Why?'

Patience closed her eyes. 'I like to hear you read in French.'

'I've nearly finished. It's rather sad.'

'Please?'

There was a flutter of the net at the windows, as you get before a storm, in the middle of stillness.

'"*Je te désirai tour à tour comme le fruit suspendu, comme l'eau*

151

lointaine, et comme la petite maison bienheureuse que je frôle . . ."'

'What's *frôle*?'

'Touch.'

'It's not about a house at all, is it? Not really?'

'No.'

'Can I get under the sheet?'

Laura whispered. 'Take off that horrid shirt. It's too hot.'

'I'm too fat.'

'And I'm too thin.'

'You're not. You're beautiful.'

They lay smiling and yet it was quite solemn, then wordless. The girls curled together, the sheet thrown off.

Patience said in a low voice: 'Laura. Did you ever do this with Scotty?'

'No. No, I never did this with Scotty.'

'D'you think it's wrong?'

Laura lay back, her head resting on her arm, her gaze turned away.

'I used to think. Not Scotty, that was just silly fun. But I thought sometimes that I loved Heini in a forbidden way, because I missed him so much, and Stephen muddled it. Now I believe all love is good. So if God forbids it, God must be wrong. It's so simple really.'

'They make it sound dirty. Stupid old Mallard and Drinkwater.'

'Oh, I daresay God might be right about them!'

'I can't believe this is wicked. I know it isn't.'

'Ma pauvre petite anglaise.'

'French frog!'

'Suet pudding!'

Laughing, they kissed and slept until the weather-cock turned on his steeple and the sky broke, waking them, sending the workers home from the fields and Mam'selle scuttling indoors like a mouse.

'Well,' said Rose, not unhappily, towelling her hair dry by the tiny fire, 'that's the last camp for us, I suppose. And now we'll have to grow up.'

The next morning they piled into the lorry to take them to the station. This time there was no singing. The prisoners looked up as they passed, then bent again to their work.

152

Part Three

13

'It was my fault,' said Laura, 'I shouldn't have gone.'

Olga the Boots slammed down a saucepan. 'It happen anyhow-ever. Your mother crazy woman.' She blew her nose on a filthy handkerchief and, giving up any pretence of activity, sat down with the girls by the stove. They drank their tea. 'I cannot see, my eyes rain.'

When Olga had stomped downstairs, Laura smiled weakly.

'Sorry about the tea. She keeps the same leaves in the pot for a fortnight. She calls it her samovar.'

'What will you do?' Patience was as stunned as Laura. When she should be helping her, she felt so far from her. Was that what tragedy did? Divide?

'Do? Oh, I'll stay here. After all, I'm almost eighteen. Olga will keep house, as you say. It's near the hospital. That doctor . . .'

'He had to, Laura. She needs nursing. You couldn't have done it.'

Laura sat bunched as though against cold, angry, hands locked, strange, old, a foreigner: 'He thought – that doctor – those refugees, these mad people, why do they come, why do they bother our country? I saw it. It's the same everywhere. Passports please! He is the kind of man who would have imprisoned my mother.' Patience let her rage on, rocking like a lonely child, until finally she dropped her hands, exhausted, and looked up, her face entirely stripped of all but one anguish: 'Oh, Patti, I didn't love her enough!'

They sat on a wooden bench in the hospital corridor. The old infirmary had hardly changed since the great merchants, mill-owners, lace-makers – James Fleet, perhaps, among them – having

155

established themselves most solidly on earth, gave a nod to Charity, taking out insurance on heaven. Brown-painted, the crammed wards were high-ceilinged echo chambers which produced weird acoustic effects: whispers ran along the walls, sighs, groans, secrets; feet clacked from a distance and only the rubber-wheeled trolleys moved soundlessly. Even they conveyed an oiled sibilance.

Carrying their flowers from Mary Mackenzie's garden, the girls were at last told they could go in. The nurse, hardly older than they were themselves, apologised: 'The mental ward, you see. It's not like the others. We have to keep it locked. The staff shortage. And we don't have the facilities. Really she ought to be in Longmore but since the bombing we've had to put them up. She's down at the end there, behind the curtain.'

'Shall I wait?' said Patience.

'No, come. She likes you.'

Patience had expected – what? The mad scene from Shakespeare? Strait-jackets, howls, shrieks, Mrs Rochester? Nothing like that, though one girl was crying, and the few visitors seemed as ill at ease as she felt herself. Though it was not so far, the walk to the far end of the ward seemed endless. An old woman drooled into her pillow, another clung to the bars of her bed, someone laughed too loudly, a pretty girl with shining brushed hair sat up straight in her bed, drumming with her hairbrush: tap tap, tap tap. A few were walking around, in dressing-gowns without cords.

The nurse who had shown them here was gone. A male orderly stood at the door.

Sophy Meister was in a bed at the furthest corner, beneath a window that gave her a little square of sky. Patience let Laura go ahead of her.

'Maman?'

Sophy lay with her face turned away from them, her gaze fixed, apparently on that small handkerchief of blue sky. Her hair that had been so beautiful, was grey at the parting, and dry.

The next time, she did turn her face to them, and speaking to Patience, not to Laura, whispered: 'Look, you see, the window is barred. They tell me I am not in prison but you can see the bars.'

'Maman,' said Laura, 'those aren't bars. It's the paper stuff against blast – like we have at home.'

Sophy's fingers fidgeted with the edge of the sheet. She grumbled imperiously: 'Take her away! That silly girl. I do not wish to see my silly daughter.' Then, confidingly again, she hissed: 'She steals love. Lolly steals love. My own daughter! Would you believe that?'

This time Laura saw the doctor before they left. She came out of his office still pale, but a little more composed. The girls walked out into the hazy October sun, into a world of unreal peace and ordinariness.

'Can we walk a bit?'

'Let's go across to the Castle.'

They sat on a bench in the Castle grounds. A Japanese maple was in full blaze. A woman called to her child to get off the grass, then smiled, sighed.

Laura took a deep breath, then finally told Patience: 'He says it's good that she's angry. That I mustn't be upset – it's the first really hopeful sign. When they brought her in – the day we were coming back from camp – and when they could finally make sense of poor old Olga, they gathered that Olga had found her sitting in a corner of her room, with her knees up and her face pressed to the wall. Beating her head against the wall.'

'And your father?'

'He got a pass straightaway, of course, but she didn't know him either, poor Papa.'

They sat on for a while, until the sun died in the Castle windows and there was a nip in the air. Walking back down the hill on the path between the forbidden lawns, Laura said: 'It's strange what I feel, such a muddle. I know I've never really loved her, sometimes I've hated her. But seeing her like this – it's a sort of love, something to do with being the same flesh. I can't explain. Dutiful love? I don't know. But seeing her, I feel that's my blood too, my flesh in that horrid place.

'Then I think, this happened to her when we were so happy, you and I.'

Patience considered. 'I thought of that too. If we were wicked, and this was – you know – a punishment.'

For the first time that day, Laura smiled. She slipped her arm through Patience's. 'Oh! You English! You and your sins and punishments – how you ever dare to be happy, I don't know. Come on – let's make mad pigs of ourselves in the Kardomah before they shut. If we hurry, we'll just make it.'

'There's the Castle siren.'

'Not for us! Not tonight. Oh, Patti, do come on –'

The girls ran down the hill.

New term, new rules. Miss Winterton's 'cracking down' on the most trivial infringement of authority.

Gas-masks, for instance, were to be carried at all times. Officially they always had been, but no one did, of course. You hung them in the cloakroom and ran for them when there was an air-raid warning, which was hardly ever now. Nina got round that by taking out her gas-mask and using the carrier as a sort of handbag. Rose, who was trying to get over Miss Lowrie, developed an appetite to fill the gap between schoolgirl crush and hoped-for womanhood and from her gas-mask case would produce any extras she could scrounge.

Running had always been forbidden in corridors, but now there was to be no speaking in the walk from class to class, unless directly addressed by a member of staff, or senior prefect.

The powers of senior prefects to administer summary punishment were extended.

Barbara Baxter was Head Girl, by direct appointment of Miss Winterton.

Miss Winterton sat in her study, having what might be her finest hour.

'I have commissioned,' she declared, 'an old college friend to compose for us a school song! Something stirring, I think, Lucy. A song to march to!'

'A topping idea, Head!' Mallard sat with knees spread, eyes ablaze with fervour.

Miss Trott coughed, a small remark passed in her throat. She had won back Claire's favour yet at the same time Mallard had not quite lost it. Was Claire playing a game? One lieutenant against the other? Increasingly that dreadful woman was invited to their little sessions in the study – or simply barged in and was not put out. How could Claire bear it? She was so fastidious. Those *knees*!

'Did you say something, Lucy?'

'I was wondering,' said Lucy mildly, 'where exactly we planned to march?'

Lucy Trott was aware of stirrings in the staffroom, though from the weaker fry – none of them exactly revolutionaries. The Lowrie girl, in company with Drinkwater, had actually gone so far as to sound out Lucy herself. Who had not rebuffed them but pointed out that only the governors had the power to remove the Head. And if they were to be shown witness of the workings of the school, everything would point to efficiency and enthusiasm. Then there was the little Frenchwoman, who seemed particularly disturbed about the German girl.

'She has problems, you see, that are special.'

Lucy nodded understandingly. 'Yes, alas. As do so many in these times. You yourself, Marie-Thérèse. How you must miss Paris and all she means: the libraries, the culture.' From here it was an easy step to Racine and to a most interesting chat about the sources of *Andromaque* to be found in the Aeneid of Virgil. By which time the poor little soul had lost her thread, as though puss had run off with her knitting.

And through it all, for the girls, there was that strange feeling of fantasy to their lives, now they would be leaving. Leaving seemed as unreal, in a way, as the ending of the war might be. They could not imagine a life beyond it.

Not that we think about the war much [as Patience wrote to her father]. Not because we don't care but nothing too awful has happened to anyone we know. We see pictures of the bombing in London, and it's marvellous about Stalingrad but both the horrible things and the victories seem so far away. I suppose we've just grown up with it and we're used to it, like school.

Anyhow, it looks as if none of us need worry about what we're going to do because then we'll all be in it, whether we want to or not. Miss Trott keeps on about the university – she says to get accepted and go back afterwards, when I've finished being a land girl, or whatever. But then we don't know about afterwards, do we?

Rose is definitely going to be a nurse – she would have done that anyway, and Barbara can't wait to get into the ATS. I'm not sure about Nina, but she'll have to make up her mind soon or she'll just get sent into munitions. Mother's busy with the WVS, but I expect she's told you about that. It's Laura I wonder about – if they'll let her work, even in a civilian job, because of all the complications. Her mother's quite ill now. I'm sorry for her, it's dreadful, but in a way I'm very happy too. Is that wicked? Laura laughs when I say that. I wish you knew her. I wish you were here. But it doesn't hurt quite so much. Do you understand?

There was a glitter about Laura. When Olga had left for the night, they would do their homework, then read or talk, curled together in the tower bedroom or in Sophy's boudoir-sitting-room, before the small fire. Once or twice, Mary Mackenzie said Patience could stay overnight, to keep Laura company. They lay on Sophy's bigger bed – the divan upon which she had spent her legless days – and pulled the quilts and shawls around them, though by the light of the fire they could still see. And needed no light. Then the world was this very small overdraped room of winking bibelots and firelight, which diminished further to the size of the bed and their content, each recognising in the other's body their own and yet the difference between one flesh and another. Dark and light. A matter of scent and taste: sweet and sharp. Till Laura was quietened; she lost the edge of hysteria that followed her from the hospital bed. And Patience felt beautiful for the first time in her life. She loved.

It occurred to her: 'Laura, with Stephen . . . Did you ever?'

'Hush, Patti-Patti.'

Laura slept. Patience lay awake. The November wind had risen and leaves stirred in the gutters. Was it the wind or the Castle siren? Whatever it was rustled and hushed, and an immense silence followed, waiting.

Miss Trott called Laura back at the end of class. It was a January day. Miss Trott was standing by the window in the last of the afternoon light. The camp looked like a flat drawing on grey paper.

Since Christmas they had not seen the boy with the shaved head. In her odd, little bird-like way, Posy mourned him, but dared not ask the guards.

'Laura,' said Miss Trott, as though she had forgotten calling her back. 'Yes, that's right. I was thinking, Laura, that your circumstances at the moment are hardly easy. I wished to assure you of our sympathy.' All the time she talked, she kept her gaze turned on the camp.

'Thank you, Miss Trott.'

'I wondered too, if we might not find a way to ease your difficulties. You are now eighteen and your own woman. Any step you chose to take would be understood.'

Laura took a breath. 'Are you asking me to leave the school, Miss Trott?'

'With regret, we would let you go.'

Laura flushed. 'If the bank payments . . .'

'Oh, there is no irregularity there! Please understand. I mean, simply, we would not stand in your way. With so few months to go . . . Your poor mother.'

'I prefer to stay, Miss Trott.'

The teacher nodded, curtly – a dismissal too. Only when Laura had left the room did Lucy Trott turn from the window, almost called the girl back again. But she sighed, pinched the bridge of her nose, easing her spectacles, and, feeling not altogether herself, sat behind her desk, opened an exercise book. Nothing, she thought of her fleeting unease, her weariness – simply the ache of the years. She sat on in the dark.

'The old cow!' said Nina. 'Though I can't think why you want to stay in this dump. Oh well, everyone to his *goût*. Which reminds me – must run. The most divine creature you've ever seen! Sort of Cary Grant gent and Clark Gable brute all rolled into one.'

'I like Leslie Howard best,' said Rose firmly. Then, when Nina had gone, she too reached for her cloak from the peg, picked up her books, and said shyly, quite fast: 'I'll light a candle for you, Laura, and for your mother. I shall ask the Blessed Virgin to intercede.'

'Sweet Rose,' said Laura.

'Was it really awful?' Patience asked.

'I felt sorry for her in a way. She used to be nice to me.'

A power cut, and Doktor Meister sat in the kitchen teasing Olga by candle-light. Countess Olya, he called her and clicked his heels and kissed her hand and brought her once a pretty handkerchief. Made her blush, the old girl, in the muddle of languages in which they communicated. He was tired, Patience thought, he came from a secret world of which he could not speak and to which he must return; from the bedside of a wife who did not know him. But he brought light with him, fun, switched on the wireless for some music. *Last night there was a heavy raid on Berlin. Losses . . .*

'Turn it off, Papa.'

He nodded, put an arm round his daughter. 'Places don't matter, Lolly. The people, yes, those who have been trapped.' Patience, sitting quietly in the shadows, was surprised: she had hardly ever heard him speak of Germany or the war. 'Yes, we know many of good heart who were blameless but too small to say no. And others for whom it was worse, much worse. But in war a country is like a prison.' Enough of that mood, he seemed to decide, for he continued more brightly: 'Now I will tell you a story!' That, Olga did understand, and watched the Herr Doktor with the sharp, excited eyes of a child. Laura's father said: 'You remember, Lolly and Miss Patti, the famous philosopher in the kitchen garden?' The girls nodded. 'Well, for months now, he has been very secret indeed. All night he would work. Ah! thought His Majesty's Government, he is about to produce some great new propaganda weapon to bring the enemy to his knees. The rest of us awaited a statement upon the nature of the universe. He grew thin. We gave him our chocolate rations, smuggled eggs to nourish this great mind. And you know what he brought forth? Only last week? An onion! The greatest, the best, the most pest-free and magnificent onion in the world!'

Olga rose from the table, cross. 'That is the most foolishy story I heard in my life.'

Doktor Meister asked if his wife might have a private room,

however small; he had the impression that the other occupants of the ward disturbed her. It was explained to him that, since the bombing of Longmore, they had had to take not only the overflow of civilian patients, but at least two serious cases from the POW camps. Those, he would understand, in need of restraint. Ah yes, he did see, this odd little man with the neat moustache and tired eyes, who somehow compelled attention, though Sister was frightfully busy and not the melting kind. Yes, he saw exactly, smiling: private rooms for prisoners only.

Funny little fellow, said Sister, comes once a month and just sits though she never knows him. Always flowers, though God knows where he finds them. Just sits, as if he were waiting for her to wake up. You get all kinds.

'Poor man,' said Mary Mackenzie. 'Probably worse for him than her. It always is for those who are waiting. She was beautiful. There was something about her. But what can one do? This power cut. Take a candle.'

Mother and daughter brushed cheeks.

Mary sat on. Her eyes were tired with darning. These spectacles, she could not get used to them. By the light of the candle, she pulled out a grey hair. Once, she would have felt Graham watching from the flat photograph. What happens? Something physical, like any organ? The heart atrophies, unused?

You have to learn not to feel [Stephen Marlowe wrote to Laura]. At least for a bit. D'you know what I mean? Gone for a soldier (well, airman), never thought I would. What helps – in between frights – is it's so ordinary, like school. Not just being told what to do and jump to it, but the other things – when you could chuck a boot at someone if he whistles the same bloody tune again. Like this morning, when I was so angry someone stole my soap – then saw how loopy it all was and laughed . . .

. . . When I said you had to learn not to feel, I didn't mean just this dump or being frightened you'll be blown to kingdom come (don't worry, I won't). I suppose I meant that I have to stop myself

163

thinking about you, and us, all that. For the duration, as they say. Do you understand? I think you will. The others pass round photos of their girls, but I've never shown yours to anyone. That reminds me: Patience was always going on about someone who was my double – do you know anything about that? Funny to remember that now . . . One thing that's good is when you're coming back, home and dry, a few miles from base, and it's a clear night, then I shove away the charts and practise a bit of celestial navigation. Always potty about stars, you remember . . .

Tiphys, helmsman to the Argonauts because he was a stargazer, Laura remembered, from some lesson or other of Miss Trott's. She pushed the letter in a drawer, not liking quite to throw it away. At that moment Stephen Marlowe seemed about as real to Laura as that distant navigator of the *Argo*.

Somehow, all the way from the desert, on a journey from hand to hand that must have taken one year, two, Graham Mackenzie had smuggled to his daughter a coin of Alexander the Great as Heracles; on the reverse side a club and an ear of corn. Patience and Laura opened the little leather sack together in front of the fire, and then the box.

'It must be very old.'

'Two thousand years at least.'

'Was it gold once, d'you think?'

Patience shook her head. Don't know. Just for that second, for the first time for how many months, she could see her big-boned father with the freckled hands, squatted awkwardly on his haunches, sifting the sand for treasure, for her.

'Oh, Laura.'

'Yes, Patti-Patti. Yes.'

Great event. School song to the tune of 'Land of Hope and Glory' bravely thumped out by Mam'selle on piano newly tuned for the event but beyond, alas, either hope or glory. Poor Elgar.

Classes had practised individually, but there were also song sheets.

Patience shared hers with Nina, who pulled a face. From the stage you could just see the tops of the Arboretum trees in their April haze of buds.

> *Sisters! all together*
> *Let us bravely ask –*

Rose, on the other side, had a pretty voice, high and clear. Posy had the sneezes. She always did in April. Barbara Baxter frowned.

> *To Die or Live wherever*
> *We are sent our task –*

From behind the song sheet, Nina hissed something Patience couldn't catch. She dipped her head closer to hear. Patience, merely mouthing the song, thought how only yesterday, a month, a year ago, those boring words would have stirred her, just a little, a breath of fervour in tune with the rest; now she felt a vacancy, an absence – the kind of blankness, she supposed, that came upon you when you no longer believed in God.

> *Help in our Endeavour*
> *He who only knows –*

But if He was, and if He really knew, then He must be a beast to let things go on like this. Nina was hissing again. Patience, with her little half belief, her left-over English Protestantism, closed her mouth and refused to speak to God. If He were listening. If He were.

> *How we reap in Labour*
> *Every seed He sows!*

'Couldn't hear. Sorry?'
'So am I. Preggers.' When Patience still seemed not to understand, Nina groaned: 'I'm pregnant, you idiot. Up the spout.'
Right on cue, in came Miss Winterton, fluting to Dada in the sky: 'And now, oh Lord, have mercy upon us, miserable sinners.'
Today, Claire Winterton did not quite believe that. Today, at least,

Dada, her beloved father who had taken his sweetness to Heaven, would surely approve?

'Boiler-room or shelter?'

'Shelter.'

'So that's about it,' said Nina. 'The divine one sowed and I shall bloody reap.'

The others sat in a glum row, looking at her. She appeared no different. In the now abandoned shelter, the roots of plants had begun to thrust tendrils down through the earth to the underground world: nettles and mint, convolvulus.

'When?' Patience said at last.

'When what?'

'When will you – you know?'

'Oh. About November.'

'Can you still do Higher Cert or will it show by then?'

'Posy. You really are a classifiable fool. Higher Cert is at the moment the least of my problems. But, yes I could do it, and no, I won't show then, or not enough to notice. Provided, that is, I can stop myself screaming or throwing up.'

'Was it the Beautiful Beast?'

'Him or the Holy Ghost. The result is the same.'

'D'you want to marry him?' asked Laura.

'Not much.'

'Oh, but you'll *have* to,' cried Rose, 'to give it a name! It's not all awful, Nina – a lovely baby! And you love him, don't you?'

'Love?' Nina lit another cigarette, pulled a face and stubbed it out.

When the others had left, Nina, Patience and Laura walked together to the Arboretum terrace, at the furthest point from the youngsters playing. Moss grew in the crevices of the balustrade and though it was too early for nasturtiums, there was a fall of periwinkle. Out of the breeze, in a sheltered spot, one of the prisoners sunned himself like a man on a beach. The air tasted warm.

'I didn't mean to be a pig to Rose,' said Nina. 'Or Posy. But I don't know what to do. I've tried everything – jumping off tables, you know . . .'

Laura pondered. 'Does he want to marry you?'

'Yes, oh yes, the Corporal is willing – but can you *see* me? An American housewife with a squalling brat? Even if we ever get to Ohio or whatever it is.'

Patience was surprised. 'I thought you said he was a Captain?'

'He *said* he was. At least, he didn't say he wasn't; they all look the same in that damned sexy uniform. It was the Palais, you see, where all ranks can go.'

Neither Laura nor Patience had to voice the other question in their minds. Nina answered it unasked: 'No we didn't. Those messy rubber things.' She grinned painfully. 'You probably don't believe me but I never have, me of all people. Asking for it, I suppose, but somehow you never think of it happening to you, only other people – like being bombed. The American Army's daftest tart.'

'Nina!' Patience was upset.

'Well, I am.' Just talking appeared to have calmed Nina a little. They walked slowly back to the classroom. After a while, Nina said: 'You know what the worst thing is? Although I can't see it or feel it – except that smoking makes me sick – I keep thinking, it's in me, taking me over. I'm not me. Just a cow carrying this lump that will be a person, inside me. The American forces occupy Nina Cherry.'

'Are you sure?' Laura asked.

'Absolutely. Missed twice. Then I bought a Woolie's wedding ring and went to a doctor, not our own.'

As they stepped out of the sun, into the shadow of the school, Laura said: 'Nina, please don't do anything – silly, will you.'

'Back-street butcher with knitting needles? No, no I promise. I suppose I'll tell my parents, marry the brute the day I leave this dump, and live somehow ever after.' They were going to different classes, and in the corridor, at the corner, Nina waved and ran off almost cheerfully. 'Bless you both,' she called.

'I'm not sure I'd really like a baby,' said Patience finally, after reflection. She and Laura were doing their homework at the Meisters' kitchen table.

'Then you shan't,' said Laura. 'We shall be two elegant and eccentric ladies travelling on the Continent. If there is a Continent left to travel on.'

'Ugh. Not like Winterboots and Trotty.'

'Not at all! You shall wear black velvet suits with long cloaks and I shall wear chiffon.' Suddenly an idea seized her. 'Look! Let's dress up now! Come on – to my mother's room, all those fantastic clothes. We can dance to her gramophone.'

'Oh, Laura, do you think –'

'Olga's not back tonight. She's taking a cabbage to some obscure middle-European relation in Leicester to make sauerkraut. Come on! Let's celebrate.'

'Celebrate what?'

'Anything! Nothing! That Olga has a cabbage!'

And so they did, up in Sophy's room. Worth and Molyneux they plundered, feathers and hats, Sophy's stale Turkish cigarettes from the onyx box, shawls, velvet, satin, harem trousers and yashmak from some forgotten masquerade; and danced to the slick tunes of Sophy's latter heyday, kissed and twirled and kicked up their heels. Patience knew the game now, Laura's games, snapped her fingers for ghost waiters to fill dream glasses, strolled imaginary terraces and gazed at seas there never were. Danced again, till there were tears in their eyes and they fell asleep, the houri and Pierrot on their fantastical divan. Till Laura woke and whispered: 'Patti-Patti, you'll never leave me, will you? Ever?'

The quietest summer. Dear father, now Tunisia's been surrendered will you be home?

The odd little foreigner still sat once a month by Mrs Meister's bed but he might just as well sit by a grave, said Sister, to whom it seemed contrary to be mad in the middle of a war. As though there weren't enough for everyone to worry about; real wounds, she'd seen enough of those. And talk – lately he'd starting talking and just went on talking to the wretched woman quietly but on and on as if she could understand; sometimes English but mostly foreign lingos – read her poetry even, that's how it sounded. No trouble as a visitor though – always so neat and polite, not like some. Only time he'd been different, she'd asked him to have a word with the German boy

n the private room – the one the camp couldn't manage, acute
catatonia – but he'd shaken his head quite sharply: you will excuse
me, please, he'd said . . .

Playing tennis, Nina suddenly went white as death, Mallard
shoved her head between her knees and sent someone for water, but
Nina wouldn't go to Matron. She's changed so much, thought
Patience; have we all? Or is it just growing up, the real person coming
out? I'm happy, that's what's so wonderful, but at school I have to
hide it. If Trotty guessed. Is she watching? No, too busy fighting
Mallard for Winterboots. I feel like Laura – sorry for Miss Trott, she
used to be all right. I'd like to show her the Alexander coin, I would
have once. Things can be spoiled, I know. Will this be spoiled?

Meanwhile, Nina had a favour to ask of Laura.

'You see, I can hardly do it at home. So really, you're my only
hope. I can come up with the gin – they're saving it for if we win the
war. Easy to swipe.'

'It would have to be when Olga was away. And Nina, are you sure
– I mean even if it works?'

'I'd be the happiest drunk in town.'

So they ran Nina an unpatriotically deep bath, reheating from
kettles as the temperature and the level of the gin bottle went down.
At first, it had been almost funny: Nina hiccuping among the rising
steam, quite gay. Then she was sick once, gritted her teeth and
demanded more kettles and lay there broiling, her head lolling.

'She looks awful,' Patience whispered by midnight. 'Shouldn't we
get her out? Nothing's happened.'

Laura nodded. They drained the bath and somehow between them
hauled her out, towelled her dry and laid her on Sophy's bed – they'd
never have got her upstairs.

'She'll have an awful hangover,' said Patience. 'We'd better stay, in
case she's sick.'

They sat out the night. Nina was sick a couple of times. She
mumbled in her sleep but in the morning she was coherent.

'I'll be all right,' she said. 'Honestly. Just leave me. I told them I
was staying the night here. Just make some excuse at school.'

'But if something happens?'

'Nothing will now. I know. If I just sleep.' She had drifted o[ff]
already, before they left.

In the afternoon when they got back, she was shaky still bu[t]
dressed, ready to go.

'Wouldn't mind a cup of tea. Did I make a frightful fool of myse[lf]
last night?'

'You were very brave.'

'I was an idiot to think it would work. Too far gone, anyway.[']

'So what now?'

'Looks as though the little bugger's decided to stay, doesn't it?' Sh[e]
grinned crookedly. 'And you know, the funny thing is, I don't min[d]
so much. Mother Nature, I suppose. Who'd be a woman?'

When Nina had left, the girls sat on at the kitchen table for a whil[e]
both exhausted by a school day after the night's vigil. Neither wante[d]
to talk. At last Patience said: 'Better clear up the bathroom and ope[n]
the windows before Olga gets back.' Laura nodded but neith[er]
moved. It was as though poor Nina had shown them something [of]
significance they had yet to fathom: in both her pain and acceptanc[e]
a view of a world, of their bodies, of their sex, to which they ha[d]
never before given consideration. And would prefer now to shru[g]
off. Laura said, in a low voice, not meeting Patience's eyes: 'Yo[u]
asked me once about Stephen. The answer is, no we didn't – wh[at]
d'you call it – we didn't go all the way. Not quite. I liked him and [I]
think I loved him a bit, because of Heini, you know, and I w[as]
unhappy, and it was like a make-believe. But perhaps you shouldn[']
involve other people in your make-believes. He writes to me. He st[ill]
loves me, you see, and I don't write back. And I think you liked hir[n]
Patti, so perhaps I stole him from you. Then my mother is right, m[y]
poor mad mother – I steal love. D'you think, Patti?'

Patience shook her head. After their night with Nina, they ha[d]
reached that point of tiredness – a little like some stages of drunke[n]
ness – when it seems important to labour after truth.

'Laura? Is this a make-believe?'

'No, Patti, I'm sure. I'm certain of that. But I don't know what w[ill]
happen.'

The two girls regarded one another gravely. It seemed a long wa[y]
from last summer at the camp, the room of white beds, *la peti[te]
maison bienheureuse.*

14

The long, feverish climb up the hill to exams. Revise. Decline. Conjugate. Dates of. Reasons for. Posy, who was taking only art and domestic science, ran from one group of swotters to another, sharing her sweet ration. Tempers were short as the air warmed and the trees thickened. Lucy Trott, suffering the annual attack upon her nasal passages, felt this year, more than ever, her age. Aches here and there, neuralgia, a distaste for this little, dangerous world; even a moth of doubt: this whole business of teaching, to which she had vowed herself, might it finally diminish one – you stay, they go – and whom did it enrich? She brushed away the night insect and reached, sleepless, for her bedside lamp, knocking Catullus to the floor. An omen? She was apprehensive. Of old age. Of something less specific? Of some hysteria building among the girls more electric than usual? Night fears. The air was heavy, rumbled, though not with thunder. Ours, she thought, a big one.

Barbara Baxter was away for three days. Her father had been killed, shot down in the raid on the Ruhr dams. The older girls were disturbed, the youngsters excited by this vicarious drama. Barbara's followers swelled in their numbers, picked posies for her return as martyred heroine. Miss Winterton was wonderful at prayers. The little ones thought Barbara looked marvellous, pale but brave, like St. Joan.

'We have to,' said Rose, and of course she was right.

In the senior cloakroom – the first time they all met since morning prayers, Barbara accepted condolences. Rose was right, Patience thought; no one's altogether awful and in a situation like this, it has to be pax. Barbara seemed to accept this. Then Laura spoke:

'I'm terribly sorry, Barbara.'

Just as though Laura had not spoken, Barbara Baxter turned on her heel and walked away, swinging her tennis racket.

The next day Laura opened her desk to find that her exercise books had been torn and soaked in ink. Her dinner tickets were missing from her locker. There were giggles, scampering feet, echoes in corridors. Then, chalked on the blackboard: *Laura Meister Jerry Go Home.*

Miss Trott stood for a moment, her back to the class. Then she turned and said calmly: 'Someone will please wipe the board. We shall then revise the causes of the French Revolution.'

That same day, Laura was struck on the back of the neck by a small stone. There was very little blood.

Dazed with headache, Lucy Trott saw Claire Winterton, seated at her desk with her back to the big window, from a great distance. She shaded her eyes (did Claire place herself there on purpose? to dazzle?).

'I have seen hens in a farmyard,' she said with disgust. 'All can peck one to death.'

Claire raised her eyebrows. Could Lucy be changing her tune? She hadn't been looking at all well lately, no longer what you might call a strong right arm.

'I blame myself,' Claire sighed, 'this is what I foresaw and most feared.'

'Are you saying, Claire, that Laura Meister killed Barbara Baxter's father?'

'My dear Lucy!' The Head inclined slightly forward and folded her pale hands in an attitude of prayer found often among supplicating saints – not prayer exactly, but doves' wings folded. 'We have agreed, more than once, that her influence was disturbing; she made a pretty little actress, she is a clever child, but you yourself lately –'

'Asked her to go.' The headache now was quite terrible. Only by absolute stillness could Lucy support it. 'I think now that we owe her at least her examinations. She stands a good chance of matriculation with distinctions. She could, of course, work at home, but conditions there, I gather, are not – satisfactory. I suggest that we give her a room of her own to work in. One of the little attics at the top would be suitable. They are never used.'

The Head opened her hands, gave in. After all, she could spare

Lucy a whim at least. 'But she will not mix. That must be understood. For her own protection. And now, Lucy dear, if you are leaving, would you ask Josephine Mallard to step in?'

'*La pauvre petite*,' confided Mam'selle. '*C'est épouvantable*. Quite terrible.'

Violetta Lowrie agreed. But what could one do? Nowadays so many things were terrible. And here came Drinkwater, all teeth and concern. Rising, Violetta suddenly remembered a handkerchief she had dropped somewhere.

'So that's it,' said Laura. 'At least I can revise in peace.'

Rose was angry. 'They're sending you to Coventry!' Laura looked puzzled. 'I mean, you're not supposed to be with the rest of us. And Barbara Baxter's told her gang not to talk to you. And she'll probably do something awful to anyone who does.'

'Then no one must. That would be silly. I'll be all right – they're not going to lock me in. It's only a few weeks.'

'But it's just as though *you* were to blame!'

'Perhaps I am.'

'Laura! Whatever for?'

'For being different,' said Laura quietly.

Only then did Patience look up – a flick of a glance between the two girls – and then quickly away.

I keep wondering if this is like the time Mrs Meister was ill first, if Laura is having to pay for something we should not have done, for the way we have been happy. That's why I think: I want to see her so much, to talk about all this, to be with her, but I mustn't for a while. And all the time I'm waiting for her to say, come on, you English and your guilts! Laugh me out of it.

Or could it be something worse and much more difficult to understand? Patience saw the blue cornflowers her mother had set in the middle of the polished dining-table and remembered another blue flower, in the art room, when Rose had gone for the Baxter gang, defending Laura, and she, Patience, had done nothing. She recalled too, sitting in the shadows, hearing Doktor Meister speak of the small people of good heart who were blameless but could not say no.

But she was not blameless because in this little world of the school, she was not small, she could speak, act. The others – that was Nina and Rose – were puzzled, she could tell, by her silence. Patience sat up late over her revising. She was tired, her mind was muddled by revolutions and subjunctives. Women 'like that', Laura's Scotty had said, were often lonely. Were she and Laura women like that? Was it discovery she feared?

Her mother came downstairs, knotting her dressing-gown cord. Yes, it was too late, Patience was nearly asleep. Mary Mackenzie straightened a cushion, picked up an empty cocoa mug, switched off the lamp and opened the curtains.

'Such a moon. Look how white the saxifrage is – it shines.'

Patience came up to the window, beside her mother.

'There's nothing else worrying you, is there? Besides exams?'

'No. Really.'

Her mother nodded. The dry kiss. Patience went up to bed. Mary stood on at the window, looking out at the moon-drenched garden. Wondering.

Laura was 'excused' prayers. The geography of the school – legacy of James Fleet together with modern fire-escape regulations – was such that she could, if she wished, reach her little work-room entirely unobserved. It was not so bad. It was quiet. It was the topmost room in the entire edifice. From a small round window she could see over the trees of the Arboretum right into the camp. From this bird's eye view it was like peering down into a roofless doll's-house. The men, very tiny, walked about: animated toys. Laura felt she could almost reach down and pluck one out – imagined the kicking doll-legs, waving arms. At that moment a midget-man looked up and the light caught his spectacles. A signal flashing? Absurd. He couldn't see her, she was in shadow. But Laura waved.

She sat at the table they had provided, which bore still the circular stain of a ewer or jug. A maid would have used that when Albert Lodge was a grand house. The roof sloped – at one end nearly touching the floor; floorboards were bare of all but a thin rug. It was surprisingly difficult to work alone, after all. Propped on the narrow shelf at the end of the room where one could stand upright was a jagged piece of glass – the maid's mirror? Here she must have seen herself by cold dawn and candlelight. A day off sometimes, perhaps, when she made herself pretty? Had she had a proper mirror and only this shard remained? Or was she old and tired, and this was enough for a quick glance after a splash in cold water from the ewer? It was stifling up here by midday. There was a single rusted bar across the window. Laura reached under the bar and pushed at the frame, but it would not budge. Exhausted she sat down and started again on the Treaty of Versailles. There was a lock on the door, with the key inside. She got up, turned the key, settled again at the table, and returned to her history book.

Rose said: 'Well, I think we ought to go up and see her.'

'We're not supposed to.' Posy had little spurts of courage, but not many.

Nina, sprawled over her books on the terrace outside the conservatory, couldn't think what all the fuss was about.

'If she wants to she can just walk out. She's not a prisoner.'

'Then they wouldn't let her do her exams.'

'Lucky pig.'

'But she wants to do them.'

Nina groaned. 'Quelle life! I've had it. Come on, Patti, let's go and inspect the Boche at play. Some idiot's taught them cricket.' Once away from the others, Nina looked sharply at Patience. 'What's up?'

The prisoners were playing with a piece of wood and a tennis ball, but very correctly. The umpire held a small book, consulted every time a rule was in doubt.

'Nothing,' said Patience.

'You really *are* worried about Laura, aren't you?'

'Yes. No, not really. I'm just in a muddle.'

'Aren't we all. My God! Just look at that – underarm bowling. Old Cardington would faint. But you've always been the nice sensible one, Patti. And at least Baxter's gang can't get her up there.'

'I'm not sure I am so sensible, Nina. Or nice.'

Nina's glance was shrewd. 'You want to rescue the Princess in the tower – something like that? You haven't realised yet, love, have you – we're all on our tod in the end.' Nina, sitting on the balustrade, turned to look back, up at the school. From this angle, it loomed darkly above them, a threat. 'In a few weeks what a potty little place this will seem. We'll all be away and wonder it ever mattered. It didn't, you see, really. We just thought it did.'

'I don't think I'll ever forget.'

'Come on. Back to the sweat-shop. At least I'll be the best educated GI bride in some American hamburger hole.'

'Thanks, Nina.'

'Any time.'

Sophy Meister stirred. At last she turned her gaze away for just a moment from the blank high window.

'Wolfgang?'

Serving tea at the Welcome Club, Mary Mackenzie thought of Graham. After the Tunisian surrender people had begun to speculate about a push north, into Italy. An irony, she thought, and smiled: in her mind, the longer he was away, the more she had seen her husband as a diminishing figure until he was a speck in those desert wastes. Italy though – those tumbling brilliances of flowers and blinding whites, sienna, indigo seas, soon to be spoiled – that Mary could see, though she had never been there.

Since Barbara Baxter had, to all intents and purposes, sent Laura to Coventry for reasons so unjust, it would have been reasonable and righteous to cut Barbara. But, as Patience had remarked to herself, no one's altogether awful, and in the circumstances it had to be pax.

She was thinking of this when she found herself alone with Barbara in the changing-room after tennis. To lose one's father as Barbara had – not by illness, not even a road accident, but miles away and in another country in a fashion you couldn't bear to think of – that must be terrible. And what did you say? After the first words, there was nothing left to say. There were times, especially at school, when the war had seemed no more than a story told outside, beyond the window. What had happened to Barbara's father brought it closer than any bomb-site could; as close as that desperate woman on the Coventry train.

Barbara was dressed now, but she lingered, tennis racket zipped in its cover (Barbara *would* have a cover for her racket), then said abruptly:

'I say, I didn't mean things to go this far.' She spoke quickly, as though this were a speech she had tried to prepare and had difficulty delivering. Well, I'm not going to help her, Patience thought. Barbara went on: 'It was rotten about my father, you see, and Laura is German, isn't she – and that's all I could see. I still feel like that. But then I started it and now I can't stop it. I'm telling you because you're Laura's friend. I'm sorry. That's all.'

She was gone before Patience could reply. If she could have thought of anything to say.

From her attic room Laura could hear the sounds of the school, dimly, as if through glass or water. It was like being half-asleep or ill, having asthma, and from a great distance there would be the noises of the house. She had said nothing to Olga about her present circumstances and though the old woman was sharp, she seemed to suspect nothing more amiss than the exhaustion of school-work. Father? To him Laura might have spoken, ached to speak. But he was so tired and, on his last monthly visit so happy at her mother's improvement. 'Lolly, Lolly,' he had said – 'she will be better, we will have her back!' And Olga had beamed. *She* will have him back, Laura thought, Sophy, my mother, and smiled and allowed herself to be hugged. 'I'm glad, Papa.' Olga brought up a quarter bottle of schnapps that burned when you drank it straight down.

The work-room was so hot but Laura would not ask for the window to be fixed. Patience didn't come. Laura stood on the table and managed at last to wedge open a small skylight, enough for the warm June air to flood in. If Patience would come. She looked at the sky, a handkerchief of clearest blue. She knelt by the window with its view of the camp. I shouldn't think so much about Heini, she thought. Sometimes Heini and Patience are confused in my mind.

Not Stephen. I was cruel to Stephen. I don't think of him any more. No one I don't want may come into this room. I lock the door. Patience could come in and we would talk about the games in the Berlin gardens, but then Heini was sent away. Do you remember that picnic when Maman couldn't come and Papa rowed us on the lake? The water was black and they said it had no bottom – the lake. Then Heini splashed water in my face; it was so hot, I didn't mind. The black water smelled very cold. Afterwards Heini caught a fish from the landing-stage, but it was too muddy to cook. We had sausages and slept in a log cabin in the same room as Papa. There were other people and cabins, on the edge of the forest. There was a big clearing and a bonfire, some people – beautiful blonde girls and boys like Heini – doing physical jerks and singing round the fire. Papa said not to talk to them. It was a lovely time.

I can't see Heini very well any more and I wonder if it's because he's dead. *Juliana*: I remember. Do not use *habeo* in this exercise to demonstrate the dative of the possessor: *In the Underworld the thin shades have no strength*. Our governess before Scotty read us the story of Orpheus. I was always Eurydice. I cried and she said I was an hysterical child. I stuck out my tongue behind her back and Heini put a frog in her desk.

Perhaps it isn't Heini I'm afraid to lose, but that time when I was a child?

Lucy Trott stood at the staffroom window, flung wide open for air. She could contain the sharpness of knives in her head, but suddenly her world tipped: the trees, the camp, the sky wheeled and lurched back as Lucy reached for support and found herself clutching Mam'selle's bony wrist.

'Such nonsense,' she said as the vertigo passed and she felt merely sick. 'The heat.' But trying to walk, she stumbled, and found herself steered, with amazing firmness, down the stairs and across the road.

'Marie-Thérèse –'

But the little Frenchwoman was bustling in the kitchen. In *my* kitchen, thought Lucy, a stranger, and was bothered that her things would be touched. A cup left unwashed this morning. But she was too tired, lay back against a cushion in her small and mercifully sunless room. Opened her eyes.

'Your English tea.'

Oddly laid tray. Cup and saucer did not match and instead of the Brown Betty teapot, the best and only silver in the house, never used. And now this small French person had settled herself on the other side of the hearth. How to remove her? Lucy sighed and sipped and she was, in a way, thankful.

'So foolish of me, Marie-Thérèse. My class –'

'That is arranged. I had a word with Violetta Lowrie and that will arrange itself. Rest, Lucy.'

'I am rather tired.'

Some odd dream. Scent and colour, no more than the blink of an eye and Claire in a dipped white hat talking of violets, sea.

But it was Marie-Thérèse who said: 'At our age.'

'I'm sorry?'

It must have been an hour. There was now a finger of sun on the bookshelf: soft leather spines and the green of Everyman Classics – *Everyman, I will go with thee, and be thy guide, In thy most need to go by thy side*. Scansion. Something wrong there. Always thought.

'You have had a good sleep. I was saying at our age we must take smaller steps. So to speak. One forgets. One has little pains. Old donkeys to pull traps.'

'Horses. Horses in harness.'

'Of course! Horses. But when I was very young we had in Brittany on summer holidays a trap and it was drawn by an ass. A horrid beast! But the trap was so pretty! We went to the *pardon*, and dressed him in a straw hat with ribbons. Fifteen *kilometres* on the road. The nuns were so pretty. Their hats, you know, are like paper boats with wide wings. Now you are a little better?'

'Thank you.' Strange, though Lucy, she fits this room. Perhaps I am old. I am too old for Claire's politics. 'You have been very kind.'

'Rest, my dear friend. Forget the little girls. Tomorrow will be better. That is how it goes for us now – one good day, one bad.' Marie-Thérèse surveyed her with the eye of a small brown bird, and decided it was safe to go. 'The body,' she said, leaving the remark in the air behind her, 'such a traitor. It is hard to remember one is not a girl.'

When the Frenchwoman had gone Lucy Trott sat on, drowsing. Something still worried her. She could not remember what. Finally, stiffly, she roused herself and took cautious steps to the kitchen – where Marie-Thérèse had put the tea-leaves down the sink, fatal error – to her bookcase, the leather spines molten now with the last of the sun. Touching the small objects of her life, reclaiming her house.

Treaty of Utrecht, Treaties of Vienna, Treaty of Versailles: dates, partitions, concessions, violations, consequences. Dear Papa, I am frightened and I don't know why. Patti? Is that you on the stairs? The knob turning. Patti? No – horrid goblin gigglings then muffled shrieks of laughter. Little girls. It is raining today so I closed the skylight and nearly fell off the table. Rain sounds angry on the skylight. Tried to work at home yesterday but Olga fussed, she thought I was ill. Always she wants to know why Patience does not come any more and I don't know. Consequence of Treaty of Versailles the rise of Hitler, Miss Trott says, though it isn't in the book because we don't do Hitler, he's after Modern History ends. Consequence – Papa teaching things at the university that they didn't like (Maman begged him not to), but nothing happened, except a man came and father took him into the study. They talked. The man went away and Papa was very serious that evening. He said nothing, then that we might go away and live somewhere else. I didn't mind. Then nothing happened, after all. But Heini got boring and stiff – he was always out, every evening; he found a book Papa was writing, I saw him take it from the drawer, I knew he shouldn't take it away but Heini said I was a silly child. I kicked him but he pushed me aside. Papa said you and Maman must go to Paris tonight, he would follow very soon and we must never say Heini's name again. I wanted to cry but I couldn't because of packing and the maid, and getting Maman to the station. It was better for me soon, there was Scotty in Paris and Papa came. Maman was ill then.

Every time Maman saw me she hated me because I was not Heini.
It was not my fault, was it?
All the time I could not cry.
The rain is angry on the glass.

.   .   .

As is given to the simple, Posy Potter knew things and looked up often at the high round window. She slipped a bar of Fry's chocolate cream under the door for Laura. Sometimes she just stood on that last flight of narrow stairs and listened.

The condemned observing the erection of the scaffold, they saw the desks put up in the gym. There were small disturbances, tears at home, a fainting, a feeling of being set uncomfortably apart, like soldiers. Or victims. It fretted them surprisingly that the dreaded Trotty was ill, and when she came back, not herself. Vague, almost mild. They missed the certainty of her hawk-eye and sharp tongue, even those who had most suffered. Their world was somehow out of joint.

Nina just walked straight up the attic stairs, knocked on the door, and when it wouldn't open, announced herself. She reported to Patience that Laura refused to unlock the door.

'She asked if you were there. So if you two have quarrelled, you'd better make it up.'

'We haven't quarrelled.'

Nina shrugged. 'Well, you ought to know.'

'I can't, Nina. I don't know why.'

'Up to you.' Nina went back to her books. 'You're a rum couple.'

Is this how Heini felt, thought Patience? But I've betrayed no one. I saw Laura on the way home yesterday, leaving through the Arboretum gate, and nearly called after her. But Miss Winterton was watching from her study window. Perhaps it's the exams, that I'm working too hard, but I feel I'm being watched, they're waiting for me to do the wrong thing. They don't *approve* of me any more. Something seems to have been spoiled. Maybe I'm a bit crazy. I know Nina thinks so. Is that what traitors are? Cowards? Laura is different. I am frightened to be different. Last night before the exams. Mother was very nice, though she must be worried about Father in Sicily. It was a victory, but we don't know about him yet. She said I must stop work early, so I walked to the Meisters' and knocked on the door. No one answered. I did try.

Mallard had set her stopwatch and they were about to turn over their history papers – there was the heavy tick of the clock, the shuffle of a chair – when it was observed that there was an empty desk. Mallard sighed: 'Will someone find Laura Meister? Meanwhile do not turn over your papers. I give her five minutes.'

There was a wonderful scent of syringa from the warm summer air, the world ticked on, and Patience was running from the gym, through the corridors, up the stairs and hammering at the door she should have broken down long ago. When finally they burst in Laura was found slumped by the little attic window, her wrists messily cut with a shard of glass that had once been a mirror, reflecting a face, old or pretty or young or tired.

And whose fault was that?

15

Laura was not mad. She did not turn her face to the wall, like Sophy. She gave no trouble at all, the nuns said at the small nursing home in a part of the town Patience had never visited before. Since her stay was expected to be short, it was agreed that the atmosphere in this house of soft treads and whispers and gentleness would be more beneficial than hospital. It was also a matter of discretion, since attempted suicide was still a criminal offence. In this quiet, tree-shaded house it was an offence also, of another kind, but God was ever merciful and the Holy Ghost might in certain circumstances turn a blind eye. By the nature of their work, the holy women here were more worldly than some of their sisters. Though they might intercede for the poor child, as they scrubbed and hushed and toiled, releasing into the air puffs of prayer, doves of petition to Our Lady. It was fortunate that while one fingernail of Laura's was Jewish, two at least belonged to Rome.

So Laura sat up in the white bed, with her left wrist bandaged.

Patience could not think what to do with the flowers. She sat with them in her lap, the stems bleeding on her skirt. Did not know what to say.

A net curtain was drawn across the window to save Laura's eyes from the light. She looked very thin in the bed, like a doll someone has propped up and left.

'When will you get out?'

'Quite soon. They're very nice here.'

'It's quiet.'

'They're a French order. Mam'selle came to see me yesterday. She knows one of the Sisters. I haven't heard so much French since we were in Paris. I'm dreaming in French again. I'd forgotten I could do that. How's school?'

'Exams still. The English was all right. But it's Latin tomorrow.'

'You're good at Latin.'

'Not exams.'

Laura kept her wrist still but moved for the first time, turning her face on the pillow. She smiled.

'Do you remember *Juliana*? You showed me the crib? That first day?'

'Seems so long ago. Nina's getting married next month. We're all asked.'

'Nina. Funny. She's nice.'

'I'd better go now. They said not to stay too long.'

'I get tired remembering things. My mother's much better, you know. We're going to rent a cottage to be near my father, and Olga will come.'

'Good. I'm sure that'll be much better.'

'You must come and see us.'

'Yes.'

Patience did not know how to leave.

'Laura –'

'I'm not going to do it again, you know. It's all right. You musn't worry.'

The Sister came into the room and nodded at Patience. Laura smiled.

'*Il faut partir*, Patti Patti.'

Only when she stood did Patience realise that she had crushed the flowers in her lap, every stem was broken, every bloom spoiled. The nun took them from her and she walked out, into the blinding light.

Exams. Vital that they should continue, declared Miss Winterton; no one must be disturbed by one hysterical incident. Sweet little Mam'selle could have wept for them, dabbed a tear from her eye, and sneezed. Mallard patrolled the aisles, spying for cheats. The scratch of pens, exhaustion, elation, just to be finished. Then two lolling weeks before the end of term. No homework. Those who wished, excused games. Sunbathing outside the conservatory. Nina's wedding.

.   .   .

Five months gone. The bump showed now. The registrar had trouble keeping his eyes up. Nina grinned. She wore her bump bravely, her hair Veronica Lake, and a dashing little pink hat – no more than a veil really, though hardly bridal. Her mother looked stiff, holding back tears. She had dreamed of a white wedding, in Church. Spring Gardens had been shocked. The child might heal that, though, she knew already, longed. But America? So far away. She knew the Mackenzies, of course, and smiled faintly at Patience. Mary Mackenzie had thought of coming, even wondered about hats, but decided better not.

The girls stayed together, uncertain whether to stand or sit. Nina carried no flowers and that seemed sad. They tried to pretend they were not craning for a look at the Beautiful Beast. If it had been Church, Rose would have committed a sin to come, but an office was surely different. She hadn't asked.

When it was over, it was very peculiar, as though some ceremony remained to be performed. Like a party with nothing to drink or eat. No music to leave by but a friend of the Beautiful Beast's, another soldier, took photographs on the steps until they were asked to move on by the next couple in the queue. Posy threw home-made confetti. That was pretty and lay on the steps like blossom. Then they crossed Slab Square to a private room at the Galloping Horse.

There were half a dozen soldiers, all American. Nina's mother and an aunt sat in a corner wearing white gloves and stiff smiles. The girls stood, at first embarrassed, then the drink someone had got from somewhere circulated and Rose, on the strength of gin and orange hissed to Patience that if it wasn't a Church, they weren't even married.

'They'll live in sin,' she said, 'and go to Hell!'

'Not as they're Protestants,' said Posy, 'that's all right. And he *is* rather beautiful.'

'He looks like Stewart Granger. His eyes are altogether too close together.' Rose could get tiddly on lemonade.

Then Laura, who had been quiet and pale, stepped forward and hugged Nina. She shook the Beautiful Beast by the hand.

'I hope you'll both be very happy.'

There was music and a little dancing, Nina, the brightest of them all, suddenly taking charge and pairing them off, making a party of it;

making the best of it? Patience, in the arms of that smooth American khaki, so different from the English, caught a glimpse of Nina dancing with her husband, Posy's confetti caught in her veil, and thought suddenly and bleakly: is that all? Is that all there is?

Then at last there was a little ceremony as the pair left and the girls in turn kissed Nina. Patience and Laura were the last and she clung to them for a moment. 'Bless you both. Take care.' Almost as though it were they who were leaving, not her. But she was gone, and they stood waving on the pavement for a long time, until she was out of sight, the girls in their summer dresses.

That same time, or thereabouts, Patience's father, Graham Mackenzie, was wounded in the victorious assault on Sicily. That was an accident: confused directions, a road the British had mined themselves. It was an accident too that after such a peaceful summer for the town, a German bomber, heading home towards the North Sea, dumped his last deadly egg on Albert Lodge. Since the place was empty – it was both night-time and holiday – no one was so much as scratched. Claire Winterton began at once to draw up plans for evacuation and – God willing – rebuilding, on a scale even James Fleet might have admired. They did not include Lucy Trott. The blast breached both the inner and the perimeter wire of the camp, but strangely the prisoners made no attempt to escape.

Except for Nina, who had turned her back on the place for ever the moment she left it, the girls – even those who had hated school – were drawn to the site, as they might have visited the grave of someone they had known a long time and possibly disliked.

Patience had not seen Laura since the wedding. In the soft September light they walked among the ruins where already, with the strange energy Nature brings to cover man's mistakes, weeds and wild flowers were sprouting in the classrooms, ivy, a ragged pink flower and nasturtiums run wild, tangled with columbine: as though all these years they had been waiting in the warm soil, breathing quietly until they could reclaim their earth.

Then there would be some startling evidence of human work: the blackened frame of the great hall still stood; and a chair here, there the intimacy of initials carved on a desk lid, little things. And a stooped, moving figure, like a small bird pecking for grain – Miss Trott looking for books.

Her hands were dusty and there was even a smudge of ash on her face. The girls seemed not to surprise her. She appeared shrunken, smaller than they remembered and was glad to pause for a moment, a sack at her feet.

'The books,' she said. 'They do matter.'

Patience was not entirely sure that the teacher recognised them. 'Can we help you, Miss Trott?'

'No, no,' said the old woman, patting her sack, 'I have the best.' She looked sharply, a blackbird's glance, at Laura. 'Laura Meister. You were a good actress in that play. I was unjust. You look peaky, child. It is difficult sometimes to remember. So many girls. But I remember you.'

Patience dared not meet Laura's eye, but she felt her tense beside her. Then Trotty sighed – as if the three had had a satisfactory conversation or a picnic perhaps – and moved on.

'I am retired, you know. But I keep busy. We all have our own wars. Death such a nuisance, don't you think? *Me fortem praebeo* – one tries. Girls never seen the point of Latin, but keep to it. It comforts.'

And off she went, stepping uncertainly between the rubbish and the flowers, the old woman poaching books.

Patience and Laura had met by chance. They were shy with each other.

'I'm glad your father's all right.'

'Well, he will be. Just a limp.' They walked on. 'I didn't think you'd want to come back.'

'Here? I had to, really. To make sure.'

'Sure?'

'That I could.' Laura grinned. '*Me fortem praebeo.* To show myself strong. Silly really, proving things.'

Patience kicked a stone. 'I didn't show myself very strong did I? I'd make a rotten Roman.'

'Oh, look – here's the shelter. Our secret place.'

They stood at the edge of what had been the abandoned shelter, side by side, not touching.

Laura said: 'I don't think anyone could have stopped me doing that idiotic thing, if that's what you mean.' As she talked she fingered, unconsciously, the scar on her wrist, like a woman fiddling with her bracelet; it was white now – a mark she would always bear. 'Papa wanted me to see some terribly clever and famous friend of his from Austria – a sort of doctor. Though, of course, he's a refugee at the moment. He's quite a nice old man. I felt silly at first, I didn't know what to talk about. Look – let's sit down. We can still get into the shelter.'

They slid down into what was now a nearly roofless trench – almost entirely overgrown, their makeshift door blown off but the brushwood, ivy and roots making of it a nest. There were even small evidences of Rose's housekeeping: a tin mug, a faded and sodden cushion. About the whole site there was that strange and acrid stench that lingered long after a bombing, but here, it was stronger.

'Like a grave,' Laura shuddered, but settled herself. 'Well, I just wanted to forget – everything. This doctor, you see, he won't tell me anything, if he has some theory. But apparently he'd helped Maman, so I have to go. He just asks questions sometimes, and says I must talk to him about anything at all, and when I'm not with him, I must think. I went to sleep one afternoon, just sitting in his armchair, but he didn't seem to mind. Another time I was bored and made things up – very naughty – all kinds of tales. I'm sure he guessed. But he just nodded – aha, ahum!' Laura flopped back, exhausted. She still looked ill. 'That's another thing I do. I talk too much. Olga says she'll put my head in the teapot.'

For the first time, the girls searched each other's faces. Patience saw that Laura was crying, silently, the tears slipping down her face.

'Oh, Patti, I did long for you.'

'And I never came. I wanted to. I was afraid.'

'Patti.' Laura took Patience's fingers in hers, looked down and said quickly: 'Can I tell you something? I haven't told the doktor. I feel I ought to have died instead of Heini.'

'Heini?'

'Yes, he's dead. It's confirmed. But we knew all the time. My father knew. My mother went mad lying to herself. Patti, you know what a scapegoat is? I got that from the doktor, he let it slip. That's what I am, I think. If I'd died instead of Heini, my mother would have loved me. I blame myself for that. For lots of things. Do you understand?'

'But that's crazy, Laura! You're to blame for nothing.'

'And when I know that,' Laura replied, recovered now, smiling, 'then perhaps I'll be cured. Oh – Patti – you look like a sad English dog! The world is not coming to an end. Look, I'll tell you something. When Heini and I were children and Maman was going through one of her Catholic phases – or perhaps it was a governess – and we'd run away to hide and miss Mass. Well, we were frightened of Hell, so we'd play a game. We'd absolve each other. Catholics can't do that, you know, but we pretended. Let's pretend now! I absolve you. You absolve me. There! We are absolved.'

So they sat for a while, then climbed from the shelter and stood for a moment.

'You do look funny,' said Patience, 'You've got leaves in your hair. Ivy. It's like the end of the play, isn't it, the Prozorovs' garden. No one knows what will happen next. Except that it will change.'

Then the two girls walked away, through the ruins.

16

An August day at the Meisters' cottage near the big house with the barricades – the first time they had met for two years. Accident or design, Patience was not sure, just that there had seemed to be no reason for meeting. Some thread had been broken, something lost or concluded, that afternoon among the ruins.

And now here was Patience, the Lincolnshire Land Girl, wearing a skirt for once, sitting here in the pretty garden, on impulse, among ghosts. Olga toiling in the vegetable plot, Sophy dreaming in the hammock – but quieter dreams, it seemed; she was well, though sometimes she forgot. Laura taught French at the village school and acted occasionally as interpreter at the big house. She appeared content enough, but looked to Patience fragile. Arriving late the night before, Patience had not yet seen Doktor Meister.

'Something going on up there,' said Laura, 'he left before breakfast.'

'To do with that bomb?'

'I suppose.' They sat side by side in deck-chairs, among the lavender.

'It must mean peace? It sounded a big one on the wireless this morning. Rather frightful, really, even though they were Japs.'

Laura nodded, went indoors to fetch coffee.

'Perhaps we'll have the real stuff again soon.' She sat down again in the basket chair. 'Oh Patti, it *is* good to see you!'

They had glanced at each other covertly since Patience arrived, surprised to find themselves grown-up. Now the appraisal was franker, smiling. On closer inspection, Patience decided that Laura did look better than she had, she had even caught the sun a little. But her features were more honed than before and because she had cut her hair very short, her skull seemed smaller, her eyes larger. She did look older.

Laura said: 'You haven't changed a bit. Now tell me the news.'

'I've seen Nina. She's fine. The baby's nearly two now. It was a girl.'

'And Nina? Happy?'

'You know Nina. She talked about the baby, going to America – but she was holding me off. Hardly the GI bride. But she might stick it. Rose adores nursing and will be gobbled up for a doctor's wife.' A bee buzzed in the lavender. 'And I'm going to marry Stephen Marlowe.' She thought, perhaps that's why I came, to tell her that.

A pause. The bee. A plume of blue smoke upwards from Olga's bonfire. Some sharper scent – a herb? A pause as short as a breath, and Laura said: 'I'm so glad, Patti. He's right. You're right together.'

Something unspoken. Remembered. Secrets. Secret places.

Later, they walked up the hill in the direction of the big house. They saw Doktor Meister coming down towards them. As he approached, Patience thought, he used to walk as a man who takes pleasure in walking.

He greeted Patience with delight and that funny, old-fashioned courtesy, kissed his daughter, but he seemed abstracted. The hedges on each side of the narrow road were high, but there was a break at one point, and here they paused, resting against a gate beyond which the land fell away: green fields, quiet cottages, stooks of corn fingered by the late afternoon sun – a child's picture of harvest.

'Pretty England,' smiled the doktor, tapping the gate with his stick.

'It's beautiful,' said Laura. The sky was wide and nearly white, only in the west a puff of smoky cloud. 'Papa – the news. Does that mean the war's over?'

'Very soon.'

'That bomb?'

He looked ill in the full stare of the sun.

'Yes, that bomb, our lovely bomb.'

She touched his hand on the gate. 'You're not to blame.'

He pondered, swinging his stick, then his mood appeared to lift.

'Not to blame. No. Not for my little bit. I may be forgiven. Forgive Rutherford. Forgive the scientists, all with their little ideas in their heads. How could they know? And Mr Truman – many dead, but many more saved.' He gestured towards the big house. 'Up there, this morning, so many moods. Triumph, blame, horror. Sometimes it takes the most courage to go on living. But we may all be forgiven.'

They continued their walk down the hill.

'Oh yes,' he said, walking out more briskly now, 'we may all forgive each other.' Then drily, with a glint in his eye: 'But one thing I wonder. Who forgives God?'

They were in sight of the cottage. The hedges closed around them.

Patience caught the evening train. It was a mothy dusk, earlier now. The two girls embraced. Patience hung from the window until Laura's figure, waving, diminished and was soon lost in the gathering, deepening shadows. Then she sat back as the train put on speed, picked up an evening newspaper left on the seat.

Peace, she thought. What a lovely word.